The Adventures of Robin Hood

The Adventures of Robin Hood

Edited with an introduction by

Rudy Behlmer

Published for the Wisconsin Center for Film and Theater Research by
The University of Wisconsin Press

Published 1979

The University of Wisconsin Press
114 North Murray Street
Madison, Wisconsin 53715

The University of Wisconsin Press, Ltd.
1 Gower Street
London WC1E 6HA, England

First printing

Printed in the United States of America

For LC CIP information see the colophon

ISBN 0-299-07940-6 cloth; 0-299-07944-9 paper

Publication of this volume has been assisted by a grant from
The Brittingham Fund, Inc.

Contents

Foreword

In donating the Warner Film Library to the Wisconsin Center for Film and Theater Research in 1969, along with the RKO and Monogram film libraries and UA corporate records, United Artists created a truly great resource for the study of American film. Acquired by United Artists in 1957, during a period when the major studios sold off their films for use on television, the Warner library is by far the richest portion of the gift, containing eight hundred sound features, fifteen hundred short subjects, nineteen thousand still negatives, legal files, and press books, in addition to screenplays for the bulk of the Warner Brothers product from 1930 to 1950. For the purposes of this project, the company has granted the Center whatever publication rights it holds to the Warner films. In so doing, UA has provided the Center another opportunity to advance the cause of film scholarship.

Our goal in publishing these Warner Brothers screenplays is to explicate the art of screenwriting during the thirties and forties, the so-called Golden Age of Hollywood. In preparing a critical introduction and annotating the screenplay, the editor of each volume is asked to cover such topics as the development of the screenplay from its source to the final shooting script, differences between the final shooting script and the release print, production information, exploitation and critical reception of the film, its historical importance, its directorial style, and its position within the genre. He is also encouraged to go beyond these guidelines to incorporate supplemental information concerning the studio system of motion picture production.

We could set such an ambitious goal because of the richness of the script files in the Warner Film Library. For many film titles, the files might contain the property (novel, play, short story, or original story idea), research materials, variant drafts of scripts

Foreword

(from story outline to treatment to shooting script), post-production items such as press books and dialogue continuities, and legal records (details of the acquisition of the property, copyright registration, and contracts with actors and directors). Editors of the Wisconsin/Warner Bros. Screenplay Series receive copies of all the materials, along with prints of the films (the most authoritative ones available for reference purposes), to use in preparing the introductions and annotating the final shooting scripts.

In the process of preparing the screenplays for publication, typographical errors were corrected, punctuation and capitalization were modernized, and the format was redesigned to facilitate readability.

Unless otherwise specified, the photographs are frame enlargements taken from a 35-mm print of the film provided by United Artists.

In theory, the Center should have received the extant scripts of all pre-1951 Warner Brothers productions when the United Artists Collection was established. Recent events, however, have created at least some doubt in this area. Late in 1977, Warners donated collections consisting of the company's production records and distribution records to the University of Southern California and Princeton University respectively. The precise contents of the collections are not known, since at the present time they are not generally open to scholars. To the best of our knowledge, all extant scripts have been considered in the preparation of these volumes. Should any other versions be discovered at a later date, we will recognize them in future printings of any volumes so affected.

Tino Balio
General Editor

Acknowledgments

The following individuals were of considerable help in various ways to the editor: Albert Cavens, Susan Dalton, George Korngold, James Morehead, Herbert S. Nusbaum (MGM), Irving Rapper, Lee Reem, Paula Sigman, and Berni Valentine.

I wish to acknowledge Robert Knutson and his first-rate staff in the Department of Special Collections, Doheny Library, University of Southern California; the library at California State University–Chico, which supplied microfilms of the *Chico Enterprise* and the *Chico Record* of 1937; and the Warner Research Collection of the Burbank Public Library.

Finally, my special thanks go to Carl Stucke, who for many years was a story editor at Warner Brothers. His aid and interest in this project were invaluable.

R. B.

Introduction: *From Legend to Film*

Rudy Behlmer

While working as a costume and set consultant on Warner Brothers' *Captain Blood* in 1935, period authority Dwight Franklin sent a memo on July 19 to studio head Jack L. Warner: "Don't you think Cagney would make a swell Robin Hood? Maybe as a follow-up to the [*Midsummer Night's*] *Dream*. With the gang as his Merry Men. McHugh, Jenkins, Alexander, Herbert, etc. Entirely different from the Fairbanks picture. I have a lot of ideas on this if you are interested."[1]

Franklin's suggestion came at an opportune time. After accumulating losses of thirty-one million dollars during the bleakest years of the Depression, 1931–34, the studio was beginning to show a profit. In addition, Jack Warner and Hal B. Wallis, his associate executive in charge of production, were in the process of changing the image of Warner Brothers. In the early 1930s, most of the studio's feature films were drawn from contemporary themes, many actually based on news stories. Epics, literary masterpieces, and spectacles—other than some Busby Berkeley musical production numbers—were shunned. But in early 1935, Warners undertook the expensive and prestigious Max Reinhardt version of *A Midsummer Night's Dream*, the antithesis of *all* of the studio's product over the previous few years. *Captain Blood*, a swashbuckling romance of the type so popular in films during the 1920s, was also being prepared, with two newcomers

1. The "gang" refers to Warners contract players Frank McHugh, Allen Jenkins, Ross Alexander, and Hugh Herbert. This memo and all other correspondence quoted or referred to in the introduction are from the Warner Brothers files at the studio in Burbank.

in the leading roles, Errol Flynn and Olivia de Havilland. The costume adventure film was once again in vogue after years of suspended animation. Two non-Warner films, *The Count of Monte Cristo* (Reliance-United Artists) and *Treasure Island* (MGM), both released in 1934, had done particularly well critically and commercially and served as catalysts for the period adventure film renaissance. The "literary" or historical film was also a convenient refuge from the new strength manifested in the Production Code Administration (the Breen Office). The film industry had been under considerable fire during the early 1930s for presenting, in contemporary settings, excessive sex and violence on the screen. Pressure groups forced a new and tougher censorship.

One of Warner Brothers' biggest draws in 1935 was James Cagney. As box-office insurance and for a change of pace, he and other popular Warner players were cast in *A Midsummer Night's Dream*, the initial example of the studio's renewed interest in "prestige." Cagney was constantly trying to convince Warners to give him different kinds of roles. The idea of *Robin Hood* for Cagney intrigued the executives and was immediately pursued.

It was discovered that Warners, through one of its music publishing firms, had a controlling interest in the popular Reginald de Koven–Harry B. Smith light opera version of *Robin Hood*, originally presented in 1890. It was also discovered that MGM was planning an operetta version of *Robin Hood* for Jeanette MacDonald and Nelson Eddy, whose initial teaming in *Naughty Marietta* (1935) had just proven to be extraordinarily successful. Naturally the studio was scrambling for follow-ups. MGM had already concluded a deal with Reliance Pictures, a relatively modest, independent production company that released its films through United Artists, to purchase two treatments of that studio's proposed nonmusical version of *Robin Hood and His Merry Men* by Bernard McConville, in addition to a working outline and an incomplete first draft continuity of two other approaches by Philip Dunne that Reliance had commissioned. Producer Edward Small of Reliance had originally planned to make *Robin Hood* following the success of his *Count of Monte Cristo* in 1934, but, for reasons unknown, he abandoned the idea after considerable research and writing had been done. These script drafts are dated March and April of 1935.

In August, after working on the screenplay of Warners' *The Charge of the Light Brigade* for several months, Rowland Leigh, a writer from England (not to be confused with director Rowland V. Lee), was assigned by Wallis to prepare a script dealing with the legendary outlaw, and *Robin Hood* was officially listed as an upcoming Warners attraction with James Cagney to star and contract player Guy Kibbee to play Friar Tuck. Leigh worked with executive story editor Walter MacEwen in evolving an approach to the subject, while Herman Lissauer and members of his research department at the studio were engaged in gathering background data on the legend and the period.

Sources of the Legend

It has been impossible for scholars or historians to trace indisputably the beginnings of the Robin Hood legend, or to place him within a specific historical context. The concept of an English outlaw who robbed the rich to give to the poor was apparently well developed by the first half of the fourteenth century, and wandering minstrels, singing of his exploits, elaborated through the years what originally was probably a simple tale. The first direct reference in literature or historical writing to such a robber-chief was in William Langland's allegorical poem *Piers the Plowman* in 1377, and ballads dealing with Robin and his merry men began to be printed by the close of the fifteenth century or the beginning of the sixteenth century.

Considerable evidence suggests that Robin Hood was, in fact, based upon the memory of one or a number of outlaws operating in the area of Barnsdale in Yorkshire about forty miles from Sherwood in Nottinghamshire. The town of Nottingham remains consistent in the early ballads, but Robin's exploits long before the end of the Middle Ages were identified with both Barnsdale and Sherwood. In the evolution of the legend, Barnsdale eventually gave way almost exclusively to Sherwood, one of the most famous of English forests in all periods.

As to reliable evidence that Robin existed and participated in events involving King Richard the Lion-Heart and his brother, Prince John—there is none. In fact, few modern historians have favored a twelfth-century date. In their exhaustive study of the English outlaw, R. B. Dobson and J. Taylor say that

not one of the many attempts to identify a historic Robin Hood in the period before 1300 carries conviction. . . . The same argument applies much more forcefully to the famous belief, first recorded by John Major [in 1521—without any valid evidence] and later popularized by Anthony Munday [in his two Elizabethan plays, *The Downfall of Robert, Earl of Huntingdon* (1601) and *The Death of Robert, Earl of Huntingdon* (1601)] and Sir Walter Scott [in the novel *Ivanhoe* (1819)], that the historical Robin Hood flourished during the reigns of Richard I and John. For this view there is no evidence whatsoever; all allowances made for the possible longevity of oral traditions in medieval England, it is hard to associate any of the incidents or references in the surviving ballad literature with a period as early as the 1190s.[2]

We know for certain that Robin and Little John were stock characters in the May Games of the sixteenth century because the outlaws' adventures were already famous in village and town. It was also inevitable that Robin would participate in the well-established morris dances. Dobson and Taylor say, "It was here that he encountered and later assimilated into his own legend the jolly friar and Maid Marian, almost invariably among the performers in the early sixteenth-century morris dance."[3] Apparently Friar Tuck is a fusion of two different friars: an actual renegade English outlaw who assumed the name Frere Tuk and the almost always anonymous and buffoonlike "frere" of the morris dances. Little John, one of the first and best known of Robin's companions, was mentioned in conjunction with the outlaw as early as 1341.

In *Ivanhoe*, Robin Hood is a key character amid both actual historical personages and fictional creations. And in 1883, Howard Pyle fused material from many of the ancient ballads for a prose collection that inspired scores of other writers to do the same.

2. R. B. Dobson and J. Taylor, *Rymes of Robyn Hood: An Introduction to the English Outlaw* (Pittsburgh: University of Pittsburgh Press, 1976), pp. 15–16.
3. Dobson and Taylor, *Rymes of Robyn Hood*, p. 41.

Introduction

The Douglas Fairbanks Film

The earliest motion picture treatments of the character were *Robin Hood* (Kalem, 1908), a one-reel American production about which little is known, and *Robin Hood and His Merry Men* (Clarendon, 1908), a one-reel British film in which the outlawed earl of Huntingdon (Robin Hood) goes to Sherwood Forest with Maid Marian and gathers his band to fight injustice. Various British and American films on the subject followed, including two 1913 versions of *Ivanhoe*, in which the redoubtable Robin (or "Locksley") is present.

In 1922, Douglas Fairbanks, flushed with his success in *The Mark of Zorro* (1920) and *The Three Musketeers* (1921), began a grandiose *Robin Hood*, which physically was the biggest film undertaking since D. W. Griffith's *Intolerance* (1916). At a cost of $1,500,000,[4] it was the most expensive film made up to that time. A huge castle was built at the Fairbanks-Pickford Studio on Santa Monica Boulevard in Hollywood (now the Samuel Goldwyn Studio). An army of experts—with Fairbanks as the guiding light—conceived and executed a vast, sprawling account of medieval England during the reign of Richard the Lion-Heart, who, at the beginning of the film, is preparing to embark on the Third Crusade with his trusted friend the earl of Huntingdon (Fairbanks). Wallace Beery played Richard.

The first half of this eleven-reel film consists of medieval pageantry, tournaments, court life, the trek to Palestine to defend the Holy Sepulchre, and treachery involving the king's brother, Prince John (Sam de Grasse), and Sir Guy of Gisbourne (Paul Dickey). Lady Marian Fitzwalter (Enid Bennett) sends word of the treachery to the earl of Huntingdon. He returns to England, learns that Prince John has usurped the throne and is oppressing the people, and dissolves into the character of Robin Hood, who, with his band of followers, sets out to thwart John and his minions until the return of Richard.

It is in the second half of the film that Fairbanks as Robin climbs the chain of the drawbridge at Nottingham Castle, leaps from battlement to tower, slides down a huge drapery, and en-

4. According to the corporate records of United Artists.

gages in feats of archery and swordsmanship. The pomp and stateliness of the early portions of the film gave way to the free spirit of "Doug," but he was still somewhat subdued by the spectacular decor.

Almost nothing from the legend is in this version. Will Scarlet, Friar Tuck, and other familiar figures are present but in relatively unimportant roles (other than Little John, who in the first half of the film is Huntingdon's squire). The accent is on sweep, romance, chivalrous deeds, and acrobatics. The script was concocted by Fairbanks, Lotta Woods (scenario editor), and others, including Edward Knoblock. It was credited to "Elton Thomas," Fairbanks's pseudonym.

As historian Jeffrey Richards has said, "Visually the film is pure nineteenth-century Romanticism. . . . Similarly the pure and noble concept of chivalry is a product of Scott [*Ivanhoe*] and Tennyson [*The Foresters*] rather than of the actual Middle Ages. Textually the film comes close to Munday."[5] Anthony Munday was an Elizabethan dramatist who did unquestionably the most influential of all pieces of dramatic writing about Robin Hood and was responsible for changing the ideal yeoman of the ballads into the unjustly dispossessed noble, the earl of Huntingdon. He also blended some aspects of the legendary Robin Hood ballads and historical events of Richard's reign—as told by Holinshed and Grafton in their chronicles—together with Michael Drayton's historical poem *Matilda, the Fair and Chaste Daughter of Lord R. Fitzwater* (1594), which involved Matilda (Marian) with Prince John. Munday then had this Norman lady fall in love with Robin and go to Sherwood with him.

Actually, neither Maid Marian, Lady Marian, nor Matilda Fitzwater (later Fitzwalter) was included in the very early Robin Hood ballads. Indeed, no romantic attachment was mentioned for Robin in the ballads until one very late inclusion from the seventeenth century titled "Robin Hood and Maid Marian." Dobson and Taylor tell us that "Marian's own literary ancestry remains extremely controversial, but it is virtually certain that

5. Jeffrey Richards, *Swordsmen of the Screen: From Douglas Fairbanks to Michael York* (London: Routledge and Kegan Paul, 1977), p. 195.

by origin she was the shepherdess Marion of the medieval French *pastourelles*, where she was partnered by the shepherd Robin. . . . It is therefore highly probable that their names and functions were later transferred to the English May Games, where they became confused with the indigenous medieval outlaw characters."[6] In his early notes on the approach to the 1938 version, writer Rowland Leigh went so far as to say: "I would strenuously put forth the suggestion in this case either that Maid Marian be omitted completely, in that she is a later . . . addition to the story of Robin Hood, or that she be brought in as little as possible, because women had no place in the scheme of life of Robin Hood and his band of merry men."

First Versions of the Screenplay

In November 1935, three months after Leigh had begun work on the *Robin Hood* script, James Cagney, in a contractual dispute with Warners, walked out and did not return to the studio for two years. *Robin Hood* was put on the back burner, although research continued, along with Leigh's work on a treatment. In April 1936, Walter MacEwen presented Hal Wallis with the first forty pages of Leigh's *Robin Hood* script. In an accompanying memo, MacEwen stated that "the great difficulty is to use as much of the traditional Robin Hood stuff as possible, without having it appear episodic and disjointed, but I think Leigh is on the right track now. The language to be used was another problem; Leigh has evolved a good modification of the actual language of the period, but it may be possible to modify it still further if you feel the need. You will find a liberal use of ballads of the period throughout the script, and if you like this, the music that goes with them should help the feeling of the picture."

Also in April, the studio announced that *Robin Hood*, previously planned for Cagney, would now star Errol Flynn. Flynn had scored strongly in *Captain Blood*, released only a few months earlier. Then in May, an agreement was concluded whereby MGM gave Warners the two Bernard McConville treatments, the Philip Dunne outline and continuity acquired from Reliance

6. Dobson and Taylor, *Rymes of Robyn Hood*, p. 42.

Pictures, and the right to make a straight dramatic picture *without singing* to be called *The Adventures of Robin Hood*, which had to be released before February 14, 1938. In turn, MGM acquired from Warners all its right, title, and interest in the de Koven–Smith operetta version of *Robin Hood*, with the provision that its release be withheld until at least the end of 1939.

In November 1936, Leigh finished his first draft continuity. Apparently Wallis did not read it until the following March. In a memo to Henry Blanke, who had been assigned as associate producer (or supervisor, as the function was called then) in June 1936, Wallis said:

I read the script of *Robin Hood* and I am frankly not too enthusiastic about it. . . . The position of Sir Guy and his connection with the Regent, Prince John, is not made clear in the early sequences. The development of the romance between Marian and Robin is too quick. . . . The episodes leading up to Robin becoming an outlaw do not seem important enough. . . . It seems to me that in this story they will expect to see Robin in action—robbing the rich, giving to the poor, and doing things for which the character was famous. . . . The most important matter is that of the dialogue. This is too poetical and too much like *Midsummer Night's Dream*. . . . You cannot have the maid or anyone else reading lines such as, "Oh M'Lord, tarry not too long for, I fear, in her remorse, she may fling herself from the window—some harm will befall her, I know!" . . . This may be all right if we were doing the picture as an operetta, but as a straight movie it won't do.

In this version, Robin (Robert of Locksley) is the yeoman described in the earliest ballads, not the Saxon knight (Sir Robin of Locksley) presented in later drafts of the script. Lady Marian Fitzwalter (Maid Marian) is the ward of Sir Guy of Gisbourne (a character in one of the old ballads), who is a rival for Marian's affection. This triangle was not a part of the legend but was introduced in a considerably different manner in the de Koven–Smith light opera, and a variation was later used in a 1912 Eclair film version of the Robin Hood legend and in Fairbanks's elaborate 1922 film with even more variation.

Many of the characters and incidents Leigh used were included in the later drafts of the script by other writers, although the connective tissue and dialogue are considerably different in the Leigh version. There is the basic enmity of the Normans and the Saxons, drawn mostly from Scott's interpretation in *Ivanhoe*, which many scholars say did not exist as late as the end of the twelfth century. The Norman conquerors and the conquered Anglo Saxons of 1066 were supposedly well assimilated by the time of Richard the Lion-Heart's capture by Leopold of Austria (1192).

In other aspects of the Leigh draft, Robin meets Little John and they bout with quarterstaves on a log spanning a stream (derived from the ballads); Robin and his men attack the royal ransom caravan, and later they feast in the forest (both suggested in part by the ballads); the archery tournament takes place, during which Robin splits an opponent's arrow (from one of the earliest recorded ballads); Robin is captured and then rescued from hanging by his band; King Richard comes to Sherwood Forest disguised (also from one of the earliest recorded ballads); and Robin and Sir Guy duel to the death at Nottingham Castle (suggested somewhat by an old ballad). The spectacular climactic siege of Nottingham Castle by King Richard and his army and Robin and his men in Leigh's version takes place for the most part outside the castle with catapults, hurling javelins, and stone throwers covering the advance while archers on the battlements unleash showers of arrows at the oncoming foe, then later pour molten lead and oil as a huge movable tower approaches the castle. The sequence suggests nothing from the Robin Hood ballads, but could have been inspired by the battle of Torquilstone Castle from Scott's *Ivanhoe*, which is a vivid depiction of a massive medieval siege. Robin Hood—or "Locksley"—participated with his band, along with King Richard, in the assault on the castle.[7]

In April 1937, contract writer Norman Reilly Raine was assigned to rewrite the script. He had recently collaborated on the

7. At least one of the prose versions of *Robin Hood*, Edith Heal's 1928 volume, features a siege of Nottingham Castle more or less as outlined in the Leigh draft. Much of what has been incorporated into the various retellings and filmings of the Robin Hood tradition in the nineteenth and twentieth centuries derives from Sir Walter Scott's interpretation of the material and the period in general in *Ivanhoe*.

screenplay for Warners' prestigious *The Life of Emile Zola* (1937). Raine was given the story material acquired from MGM as well as the Leigh continuity and the studio research data for reference and possible use.[8] On May 18, MacEwen, in behalf of Jack Warner, requested that Raine "keep color in mind when rewriting the script. When we originally started on *Robin Hood* it was not contemplated as a Technicolor production. But now . . . Mr. Warner wants to be sure that every advantage is taken of the color medium."

Although Raine's first draft (dated July 7, 1937) shows his own approach and dialogue for the most part, it does reflect ideas he assimilated consciously or unconsciously from Leigh, Dunne, and McConville (and naturally other writers of Robin Hood books, plays, and films). It is interesting to note some of the major similarities and differences in the various scripts. Bernard McConville's two treatments portray Robert, earl of Locksley and Huntingdon, as a Saxon noble described by McConville in his notes as "*not* a highway robber, but an *emancipator*." Marian, a Saxon rather than a Norman lady, is the ward of Sir Guy of Gisbourne, who is in love with her. The Norman-Saxon enmity is present. Robin escapes from the banquet at Nottingham Castle and is declared an outlaw. Will of Gamwell (Will Scarlet) is Robin's cousin (in the ballads, he is sometimes referred to as his cousin and more often as his nephew). Included are the traditional meetings with Little John and Friar Tuck; the capture in Sherwood by Robin's band of the Norman treasure caravan and the feast in the forest; the archery tournament; Robin's scaling the walls of Nottingham Castle to Marian's balcony for a love

8. Leigh had begun work on his version in August of 1935. It was not until May 1936 that the Reliance via MGM material was available to Warners. Since Leigh did not complete his first draft until November 1936, it is logical to assume that he did use the Reliance-MGM material later in the reworking of his script, but story editor Walter MacEwen in a memo (February 1938) to Ray Obringer, head of the legal department of the studio, stated that the Leigh script "was developed prior to any deal we made with MGM, and which contained, in one form or another, practically all of the action or business referred to, which was used as a result of original research by Rowland Leigh and myself prior to our deal with Metro, and prior to [associate producer Henry] Blanke taking over the assignment with Norman Reilly Raine as writer."

scene; Robin's rescue from the hangman's noose by his men; and Marian's rescue from the altar where she is about to be married by force to Sir Guy. Marian then stays in Sherwood until she, in turn, is abducted by Sir Guy and his men; King Richard comes to Sherwood in disguise; there is a major siege of Nottingham Castle by Richard and his army and Robin and his band, climaxed by the duel between Robin and Sir Guy; then Maid Marian is rescued, and Prince John surrenders. Robin and Marian are married in Sherwood by Friar Tuck with King Richard the honored guest.

Philip Dunne's working outline contained many of the same elements but excluded Sir Guy completely. In his version, there is an emphasis on Prince John's plan to collect Richard's ransom but to use it to enable John to seize the realm. This idea and that of a tax-gathering montage were consciously or unconsciously appropriated into much later versions of the script, along with Robin's appearing at the Nottingham Castle banquet and accusing Prince John of attempting to usurp the throne. In Dunne's version, after the usual adventures and the return of Richard to England, Robin goes off to fight on foreign soil as lieutenant to his king, having lost Marian to his rival, Sir Henry of the Lea. Sir Henry was a fictional creation of Dunne's having no basis or counterpart in any of the Robin Hood literature or previous films, although a character with the same name appeared briefly in Howard Pyle's famous Robin Hood book. Many years later, after King Richard is killed, Robin returns to find England in turmoil again. He rounds up the old band and eventually is delivered to King John as a hostage in exchange for the latter's agreeing to sign the Magna Carta! Robin later suffers from a fever and King John's private physician bleeds him—but far too long on John's orders—and Robin dies in a manner similar to that described in the old ballads.[9]

9. Dunne's other approach, called the Matilda Version, of which only the first half apparently was written, is alien to almost everything in the Robin Hood tradition. Princess Matilda was the eighteen-year-old daughter of England's Henry I. For the purpose of this story, the earl of Huntingdon (Robin) and Little John go to court after Henry I dies. Matilda and Robin fall in love, but the nobles try to thwart the romance because it would mean a Saxon on the throne again.

Raine's First Draft and Revisions

In Norman Reilly Raine's first draft, Robert of Locksley is a Saxon freeman who has been proclaimed an outlaw by Sir Guy. Robin is already in Sherwood as this approach begins. Marian is a Norman lady who was the ward of King Richard before he left on the Third Crusade. Robin is not present at the banquet at the castle—called Hagthorn Castle rather than Nottingham Castle—but Sir Will of Gamwell (later Will Scarlet), a Norman knight, performs the same function since he dares to challenge Prince John with such lines (some familiar to students of the film) as "I've a stomach for honest meat—but none for traitors! . . . You've used your brother's misfortune to seize his power—and for that you're a traitor, and so is every man here who gives you allegiance! . . . Of course, *you* may talk of paying the king's ransom . . . but it's the serfs who will pay; the Saxon hinds, eh?" Prince John bellows "Take him!" but Sir Will escapes from the castle and later joins Robin's band in Sherwood.

Some of the scenes in Robin Hood's camp were designated in this draft to take place at night with bonfires supplying illumination. They were changed to day scenes following a budget meeting, thereby saving about fifty thousand dollars. The biggest night scene was to be the climax of the picture, which in this version is the attack on the tax-gathering caravan in Sherwood, following which a knight in Robin's camp reveals himself to be King Richard. The king knights Robin, and the last scene is the marriage of Robin and Marian in the forest.

On June 25 Raine sent a memo to Blanke saying that he "was not satisfied with the present ending [in the forest]; and it is not the one I first intended to use; but due to the rush of getting the script finished . . . there was not time to give to the intended ending that care which it justified, so will have to delay it. . . . If the present one is satisfactory it will have the added merit of being less expensive to produce, as the original ending entailed the storming, capture, and burning of Hagthorn Castle."

On July 6 Wallis wrote to Blanke that "the budget on *Robin Hood* according to the last script [the Rowland Leigh version] is $1,185,000. . . . Of course, we cannot have a budget of this kind on the picture and in our rewrite let us bear this in mind and work towards the elimination of the huge mob scenes that were called for in the original script."

After story conferences with Wallis, Blanke, and William Keighley (a staff director assigned to the picture), Raine worked on a revision of his first script. Dated August 6 with additions through August 20, the draft went only as far as Robin's imprisonment following the archery tournament. This time the hero is introduced as a Saxon noble, Sir Robin of Locksley. Will of Gamwell is his squire. Marian is a Saxon lady who is already in love with Robin at the beginning of the story. Her father, the earl of Fitzwalter, has a role as he did in drafts by the previous scriptwriters. As in the film, Sir Robin attends the banquet at Nottingham Castle (changed from Hagthorn Castle) and escapes after defying Prince John.

Seton I. Miller, who had written the screenplay for the popular *Kid Galahad* (1937), among many others, for Warners, was assigned to collaborate with Raine on another revision starting sometime in August. On August 31, Wallis wrote to them: "I know that you are both working very hard on the *Robin Hood* script. . . . As you know, we are up against a serious problem with our Technicolor commitment which we have already postponed from the end of August to the middle of September, and it will be very costly if we are forced to postpone this again. I have been in close touch with Keighley and Blanke and I feel that the story is now properly blocked out, and if you will . . . try to get us a complete script, or at least two-thirds of it, before September 10th, it will be of great help."

It is difficult to ascertain who contributed what in the collaboration of Raine and Miller, to say nothing of the ideas that stemmed from the suggestions of the producers and the director. Apparently director Keighley put forth the idea of opening the film with a large-scale jousting tournament, which was incorporated into the first Raine-Miller version. This tournament served to introduce Sir Robin, Lady Marian (back to being a Norman and King Richard's ward), Prince John, and Sir Guy. Robin and Sir Guy joust on horseback with lances. A good deal of the expository dialogue that earlier had been included in the banquet at Nottingham Castle was now inserted at the joust (see appendix). Raine, for one, was anything but pleased regarding the value of this sequence, particularly since there were severe budgetary problems. In a memo to Wallis, Raine said it was his understanding that Keighley wanted the sequence because people remembering the Douglas Fairbanks silent feature would expect a spectacular opening sequence (the 1922 Fairbanks film began with a jousting tournament); also, it would set up and advance the story as well as illustrate the pageantry of the period. Raine said:

> People do not remember the details of the Fairbanks picture; therefore, the pageantry and color and chivalry inherent in the background itself, if we follow the revised final, will satisfy them, especially as it is to be in color. . . .
>
> The Jousting Tournament never can be anything but a prologue which, if done with the magnificence Mr. Keighley sees, will have the disastrous effect of putting the climax of the picture at the beginning—and I'll be goddamned if that is good construction dramatically in fiction, stage or screen, because the only way you could ever top it would be to have a slam-bang hell of a battle or something equally spectacular—and expensive—at the end. Maybe I'm crazy—but what we set out to tell was the story of Robin Hood—the swashbuckling, reckless, rakehell type of character who, *by his personal adventures*, has endeared himself to generations. It is not by thoughts of knights and castles and tournaments that this character has lived. . . . The Archery Tournament will certainly suffer pictorially if we stick a Jousting Tournament in the beginning. Christ's second coming in a cloud of glory would seem tame if we showed the creation of the world first. . . .
>
> The Fairbanks picture, *in order to live up to its tournament fade-in*, had to ring in the whole goddamned Crusades; and a light taste of the real Robin Hood story was dragged in as a tag at the end to justify the use of the name.

Despite Raine's pleas, the jousting tournament remained in the script for the time being.

Production Plans

Most of the cast members were set by the middle of September, as the shooting had a revised starting date of September 27,

1937. There had been some vacillation regarding the casting of Maid Marian. Originally Olivia de Havilland had been strongly considered, she and Flynn having played together in *Captain Blood* and *The Charge of the Light Brigade*. Then, in the middle of June, Warner wrote Wallis that he was "thinking seriously of putting [contract player] Anita Louise in *The Adventures of Robin Hood* to play the part of Maid Marian." In early September Wallis noted to director William Keighley that "we have decided definitely to use Anita Louise." On September 16, Wallis wrote that "Olivia de Havilland will definitely play the part of Maid Marian." David Niven was wanted for the part of Will Scarlet, but as shooting on *Robin Hood* was about to begin he was on vacation in England following his filming there of *Dinner at the Ritz* (1937). Patric Knowles, under contract, replaced him. The traditional sheriff of Nottingham from the early ballads was written by Raine and Miller as a blustering, cowardly comic villain, and Melville Cooper was chosen to interpret the role. Freelance actor Basil Rathbone was signed for Sir Guy, and contract players Claude Rains and Ian Hunter were agreed to for the roles of Prince John and King Richard, respectively.

For several weeks before production began, twenty-four handpicked men rehearsed with broadswords and quarterstaves on Stage One at Warners under the tutelage of Belgian fencing master Fred Cavens and his son, Albert, who instructed and set up the sword and quarterstaff routines for the principal players as well. The film was a boon to the stunt men. In addition to the fights with weapons, there was dropping from trees, vine swinging, high falls (Fred Graham—doubling for Basil Rathbone as Sir Guy—took a spectacular fall in the final duel and broke his ankle), and arrows plunging into padded chests and backs (the studio paid $150 per shot to stunt men and bit players for letting famed bowman Howard Hill hit them with arrows). [10]

10. Although Flynn did most of his own dueling—as did Rathbone (figure 23)—quarterstaff fighting (figure 4), and other action stunts, he was doubled on his leap with his hands tied behind his back from the gallows onto a horse (as well as an earlier leap onto a horse), his swinging ride up the cut rope to the top of the Nottingham gate, and his drop to the ground on the other side. The emphasis on stunts was in part an homage paid to the Doug Fairbanks heritage.

More revisions on the script were being made as the company was getting ready to leave for the start of production on location. On September 13, Wallis wrote Blanke and Keighley about Robin's entrance into Nottingham Castle during the banquet sequence (figure 3). In the script then current, Robin enters the Great Hall on horseback with a dead villager, who had been killed by the sheriff of Nottingham, across his saddle. Riding straight for Prince John, Robin halts at his table, slips from the saddle, lifts the body, and dumps it on the table in front of Prince John. In an earlier version of the script, Robin had entered with two members of his band, one of whom was carrying a dead deer. The deer was then dropped on the table. Wallis said that he did not like the new approach with the dead villager as well as the earlier version where Robin, after entering, sat and fenced verbally with Prince John, which led to the break between them. He regarded this as "a suspenseful scene, and there is always the suggestion of an explosion to come during the entire scene. . . . On the other hand, if he rides in and drops a corpse in front of Prince John it is a momentary kick and your scene is over."

The big dilemma with regard to the script was what to do about the climax. The exterior storming of the castle with King Richard and his army and Robin and his men against Prince John and Guy of Gisbourne's forces from the early versions had been abandoned because of the excessive cost, and the alternate plan with the final confrontation taking place in Sherwood was never satisfactory. What was needed was an exciting and elaborate finish with a fresh dramatic device that would not cost a fortune. Someone or some combination came up with a sound solution as delineated in an addition to the script of September 14: when King Richard and his retinue, who had come to Sherwood disguised as monks after returning to England (figure 14), reveal themselves to Robin and his band,[11] it is discovered that Prince John, having arranged for Richard to be murdered (figure 13), is going to be crowned king in a ceremony to be performed

---

11. As in one of the old ballads; but in the ballad the king was Edward, not Richard.

26

by the Bishop of the Black Canons the following day in Nottingham Castle. It is also discovered that Marian had been imprisoned in the castle and is to be executed for treason (figure 16). Realizing that it would be useless to storm the castle, Robin decides to visit the bishop that evening to persuade him to suggest a way to rescue Marian and stop the coronation. Fade out and fade in to the next day. Robin's entire band and Richard—all disguised as monks—enter the castle as part of the ceremony and disrupt the proceedings. After an exciting battle royal (figure 21), Gisbourne is killed, Marian is freed, John is ousted, and Richard reigns again.[12]

The new continuity solved various problems while being dramatically effective. A coronation ceremony had been the climax of Warners' recently released *The Prince and the Pauper* (1937) as well as an important ingredient in David O. Selznick's production of *The Prisoner of Zenda* (1937). Both were inspired by the much-heralded coronation of George VI, following the abdication of Edward VIII. Now, for the first time, the pomp and circumstance would be in color. Since the Great Hall at Nottingham Castle was already a key set for other sequences—most important, the elaborate banquet and Robin's lengthy escape near the beginning of the film—it was a natural locale for the coronation (figures 19 and 20), the battle (figure 21), and the concluding scenes (figure 24). Thus, an entire exterior castle set—not otherwise needed—for the medieval siege with assault towers, catapults, boiling oil, and so on was eliminated. Richard's army was also not required, and his retinue was reduced to five men.

The new climax meant the building up of what had previously been a small role—the Bishop of the Black Canons, played by Montagu Love (figure 20), who becomes involved in the evil machinations of Prince John. This bishop does not derive from the Robin Hood tradition. In Leigh's early notes regarding the approach to *Robin Hood*, he pointed out that the handling of the religious aspects of the legend could be difficult:

12. In the 1912 Eclair film, Robin and his band, disguised as monks, abduct Marian. Robin also disguised himself as a monk to rescue one of his men from the sheriff in the 1913 British Kinemacolor film, *In the Days of Robin Hood*.

There is no doubt about it that Robin Hood's chief antagonists were the bishops, abbots, and friars who bled the poor in order to enrich themselves. This point is insisted upon again and again by every reliable expert on Robin Hood lore. Undoubtedly in medieval times the church took unwarranted liberties with its power and influence. Equally undoubtedly we have no desire to offend either the Catholic or Protestant church of today, and I feel that a tactful compromise will have to be arrived at. This may possibly eliminate the Bishop of Hereford [a character in the old ballads] as the villainous character he actually is.

Joseph Ritson stated in his still indispensable 1795 handbook of the legend that "notwithstanding, however, the aversion in which he [Robin] appears to have held the clergy of every denomination, he was a man of exemplary piety, according to the notions of that age."[13] Robin Hood is the product of a period when the state was relatively weak and when local power groups could be portrayed in the form of the sheriff and the abbot. In all of the previous drafts of the script, no clergymen were included (other than Friar Tuck and the Black Bishop, who had a bit part in Raine's original draft).

The attempted coronation of Prince John with Richard and Robin and his men disguised as monks had not been used before and was not drawn from any legendary or historical source.[14]

Warner Brothers' Sherwood Forest location was a twenty-four-hundred-acre natural park filled with giant oaks and sycamores in the town of Chico, California, about 350 miles north of Los Angeles. The park runs nine miles up into the rugged and picturesque Chico Canyon along Big Chico Creek (the creek

13. Joseph Ritson, ed., *Robin Hood: A Collection of Poems, Songs, and Ballads* (London: George Routledge and Sons, 1884), p. 8.

14. In reality, at the time of Richard's return to England, Prince John was in France. Also, Richard came back to England in March of 1194, making a state entry into London, complete with a great procession and celebration. All of England was aware of his return. However, at that time it was decreed that John, having violated his oath of fealty, should be deprived of all his land in England and that his castles be seized, by force, if necessary. The surrender of the last to hold out, Nottingham Castle, was taken by King Richard himself while John was still in France. Historical records tell us that while in Nottingham, Richard visited Sherwood Forest, which he had never seen.

being the site for the filming of Robin's first meeting with Little John and later Friar Tuck). The main location in the park was Robin Hood's camp, a mile or so from the entrance. This was the scene of the outdoor feast following the outlaw's capture of the treasure caravan. Throughout the area, art director Carl Jules Weyl augmented nature by building prop trees and a number of imitation rocks to lend variety to the scenery. Hundreds of bushes, ferns, and flowers were planted temporarily and then removed when the work was completed.

The Filming and Direction

Shooting began in Bidwell Park on September 27, 1937, with the meeting of Robin and Little John. The ballad detailing the first encounter of Robin and Little John on a log spanning a stream where they fight with quarterstaves (figure 4), as well as Robin's meeting with Friar Tuck (figures 5 and 6), appeared on the screen for the first time in the Warners version. Alan Hale had played Little John in the Fairbanks picture and was signed by Warners on September 1, 1937, to play the same part. Although Guy Kibbee had been announced for the Friar Tuck role in 1935 he was no longer a contract player, and Eugene Pallette, a free-lance performer, was chosen instead.

Norman Reilly Raine was at the Chico location from late September until October 13 working on revisions, adding comedy material for Herbert Mundin, who played Much-the-Miller's-Son (one of the earliest recorded members of Robin's band), and shortening the forest banquet sequence. Things went slowly on location owing to weather and other factors. Wallis wired Keighley on October 6 about his concern that it had taken three days to film the meeting between Robin and Little John and it was not yet complete: "Don't know what you can do about it except to cut down angles and not spend so much time." The next day Wallis insisted that the jousting tournament and a christening scene of the merry men be deleted from the script to save time and money. The christening sequence was to follow immediately Robin's meeting with Friar Tuck and consisted of the friar and Robin's ducking the members of the band's heads into a cask of ale ("Name?" "Will of Gamwell." They duck him and pull him out. "Rise—Will Scarlet"). To speed things up, a second unit director, B. Reeves ("Breezy") Eason, was dispatched to Chico toward the end of October to film some of the shots of the treasure caravan, the merry men swinging and dropping on Sir Guy's party, and other material involving horse action without the principal players.

Olivia de Havilland did not arrive in Chico until October 22, almost a month after the rest of the company. She had been finishing work on *Gold Is Where You Find It*.

Nine days behind schedule, the company finished shooting in Chico on November 8 and returned to begin filming at Warners' Burbank studio on sets representing Marian's apartment in the castle, Kent Road Tavern, and the Saracen's Head Inn. In the middle of November, work began on the archery tournament sequence at the old Busch Gardens in Pasadena—long since gone (figures 9 and 10). The jousting tournament, now dropped, was to have been shot there as well.[15]

By November 30, 1937, with *The Adventures of Robin Hood* fifteen days behind schedule and over its revised September 28 budget of $1,440,000, it was decided to replace Keighley with Michael Curtiz. Keighley, an American, was a relatively soft-spoken gentleman who, before coming to Warners in 1932, had been an actor and director in the theater, working with such luminaries as John Barrymore in *Richard III* (1920) and Ethel Barrymore in *Romeo and Juliet* (1922). Since Keighley had directed *The Prince and the Pauper* with Flynn shortly before *Robin Hood*, Warner, Wallis, and Blanke had felt that he had the requisite "feel" for the subject and period. Undoubtedly another important factor in the decision to use Keighley and cameraman Tony Gaudio was that they had done Warners' first three-color Tech-

---

15. The archery tournament had been used in a 1913 Thanhouser *Robin Hood* film, but not in the two motion picture versions of Scott's *Ivanhoe*, also released in 1913—or, for that matter, in the MGM 1952 *Ivanhoe* production. In his novel, Scott has Robin ("Locksley") appear before Prince John as an entrant in an archery competition, during which the outlaw splits another's arrow. As previously mentioned, the famous incident derives from one of the earliest of the extant ballads.

nicolor feature, *God's Country and the Woman* (1937), a considerable amount of which was shot on location.

Curtiz, who had directed films in his native Hungary and in Vienna as early as 1913 before coming to America and Warners in 1926, was the antithesis of Keighley. He was tough, indefatiguable, and, according to some sources, apparently somewhat sadistic. Curtiz had directed Flynn's first screen appearance in this country (a bit in *The Case of the Curious Bride* [1935]) and the first two films in which he was starred, *Captain Blood* and *The Charge of the Light Brigade*. According to various sources, Flynn disliked Curtiz and his working methods intensely, but was fond of the urbane Keighley.

Curtiz and Sol Polito, the replacement director of photography for Tony Gaudio and Curtiz's favorite cameraman at that time, were expected to show a burst of speed and by the same token produce a high standard of quality. (They had recently completed Warners' second three-color Technicolor feature, *Gold Is Where You Find It*.) All of the big scenes in Nottingham Castle—including the banquet and Robin's subsequent escape, the coronation, and final battle—were scheduled with Curtiz on Stage One at the studio during the month of December. The director was certainly in his element. As Wallis stated in a memo to Blanke at the time Curtiz took over the direction: "In his enthusiasm to make great shots and composition and utilize the great production values on this picture, he is, of course, more likely to go overboard than anyone else, because he just naturally loves to work with mobs and props of this kind."

Wallis was concerned about Robin's early escape from the castle being overdone and appearing ridiculous: "The quicker he [Robin] gets out of the room and up on the balcony the better, and don't let him [Curtiz] have Robin holding off a hundred men with a bow and arrow, or the audience will scream, and from that point on you won't ever get them back into the story again. This must be handled very carefully and worked out very carefully."

Some of the bits of business shot for the escape were deleted much later by Wallis. At the point where Robin begins to fight his way out of the Great Hall after narrowly averting a spear that had been hurled through the back of his chair, Wallis told Ralph Dawson, the editor, to "lose the cut where he [Robin] knocks the man down and climbs up on the table and drinks the toast, and the cut of [Prince] John drinking the toast. . . . When Flynn runs across the banquet room, let him run right up the stairs and climb up over the balcony. Take out the business of grabbing the shield and catching the arrows on it and throwing the torch at the men."

By December 4, Al Alleborn, the unit manager, mentioned in his daily report that "this company with a new crew is moving along 100% better than the other crew. . . . The balance of the work that is left to do in the castle has been walked through and explained to . . . Mr. Wallis and Blanke who have approved of the way Mike [Curtiz] is to play it and the number of [camera] set-ups necessary for the action."

On December 8, Alleborn reported that "Mr. Blanke is going to discuss with Mr. Wallis and the writers necessary scenes that have to be retaken and added scenes as well to build up sequences that were shot by Mr. Keighley." By now it was considered necessary to go all-out in an attempt to make *Robin Hood* a super attraction. The costs had soared, but in order to guarantee a profit, perfection was the objective and every scene was carefully studied to determine what improvements or embellishments were necessary. This was definitely not the usual modus operandi of the efficiently run, cost-conscious Warners studio.

The attack on the treasure caravan in Sherwood was enriched by Curtiz with footage of Robin's men preparing for the attack by rigging and climbing the vines, and a few more shots of the men dropping from high in the trees, in addition to further details of the fight on the ground. These were photographed in the nearby Lake Sherwood and Sherwood Forest area, so named after being used for the forest location in Fairbanks's *Robin Hood*.[16]

16. The 1912 Eclair *Robin Hood* film contains a sequence in which Robin and his men fall upon Sir Guy's party from the treetops. In Fairbanks's 1922 production, the merry men drop on the sheriff of Nottingham's troopers in Sherwood. Edith Heal's 1928 book describes the capture in the forest of Sir Guy by Robin. This incident stems from remotely similar ideas derived from the old ballads

Additional shots and some retakes for the archery tournament in the Warners production were done later at the Midwick Country Club (Busch Gardens being too expensive and not necessary at this point), and material taking place in the streets of Nottingham was shot on the so-called Dijohn Street on the Warners back lot. The exterior portcullis of Nottingham Castle was on the top of a hill at the Warners ranch in Calabasas. Only small portions of the exterior castle were built. The remainder of the castle views were paintings matted with the full-scale fragments (figures 17 and 18). The portcullis also served as the outside of the Nottingham gate. The town side of the gate was built on the back lot Dijohn Street. Another Warner contract director, William Dieterle, photographed some scenes for a montage depicting Crippen the Arrow-maker passing the word to meet Robin at the Gallows Oak in Sherwood.

Editing and Music

Finally, on January 14, per Al Alleborn's report, "Curtiz company called 8:30 A.M. . . . finished shooting at 3:10 A.M. this morning, 1/15." The company had worked for over eighteen continuous hours. The picture had an additional day of bits and pieces one week later, which put it thirty-eight days behind schedule and considerably over budget. The negative cost, including editing and scoring, came to about $1,900,000—the most expensive picture, by a considerable margin, to be made at Warners up to that time.

MGM had consented in October 1937 to extend the Warners release date of *The Adventures of Robin Hood* from the originally agreed-on February 14, 1938, to before June 1. MGM officially announced in 1939 that it was going to produce an adaptation of the de Koven–Smith operetta with Jeanette MacDonald and Nelson Eddy, but the film never was made.

Although the Warners production had been assembled and edited while filming was in progress, final shaping and tight-

---

and an early seventeenth-century composition by Martin Parker, *A True Tale of Robin Hood.*

ening were being done immediately after shooting was completed. Then Wallis ran the edited version and made more cuts
and trims throughout, in line with the Warners practice of moving things along in a swift, staccato manner with no excess footage. Wallis's editorial notes on *Robin Hood* abound with such
instructions as:

Cut quicker to Rathbone. . . . Take out the stall before the line. . . .
Trim the beginning of the long shot. . . . After Prince John announces
that he is regent of England, make the reaction cuts all exactly the same
footage. . . . You stay too long on the man that falls. . . . Cut right to
the girl; lose all the panning around. . . . Take about three feet off the
end of that scene. . . . Dissolve quicker to the trumpeters after the first
flight of arrows. . . . Cut out that business [of Flynn] looking over the
arrow at the girl. . . . Don't have him hesitate. . . . Fade a little quicker
on de Havilland in the window. . . . Trim just a little—a few frames, a
half a foot, a foot, or whatever is necessary on all the cuts from the
shooting of the first arrow in the gallows sequence. . . . We'll shoot an
insert of a sign "Kent Road Tavern." . . . Let the scene run as long as
possible where he [Flynn] says, "And persuade him to find a way." . . .
Take out the dialogue with Hale and Pallette [during the final battle].
Just put cuts of them fighting. . . . After the jump over the table [in the
duel], go back to about two more cuts upstairs, then pick Flynn and
Rathbone up. . . . Take out Rathbone's close-up where his face twitches
in the last part of the duel. . . . Take out the line "I only pray that I have
a son to succeed my throne."

Although Warners staff composer Max Steiner was tentatively
set to score the film, Erich Wolfgang Korngold (*Captain Blood,
The Prince and the Pauper*, among others) was preferred for the
assignment. Korngold, an esteemed composer of operas and
concert works, had an agreement with Warners, but at this time
he was in Vienna completing and arranging for the premiere of
his new opera, *Die Kathrin*. Then in mid January 1938, he discovered that the premiere would be delayed until fall. When the
studio learned of the postponement, Wallis and Blanke cabled
him to come back immediately for *Robin Hood*. Upon his return,
the edited work print was screened for him at Warners. A day or
two later, on February 11, Korngold wrote Wallis turning down
the assignment. He said in part, "*Robin Hood* is no picture for

me. I have no relation to it and therefore cannot produce any music for it. I am a musician of the heart, of passions and psychology; I am not a musical illustrator for a 90% action picture." The next day Leo Forbstein, head of Warners' music department, arrived at the Korngold residence at the urging of Warner, Wallis, and Blanke and implored him to take the film. When Forbstein said that Korngold could work on a weekly basis and could leave the project at the end of any given week, in which case someone else might finish the score, Korngold agreed. What prompted him to change his mind was hearing that Chancellor Kurt von Schuschnigg of Austria had his ill-fated meeting with Adolf Hitler at Berchtesgaden. Shortly afterward, Korngold's property in Vienna was confiscated by the invading Nazis.

Korngold had seven weeks to compose and record a score that was to be wedded to the picture in time for its new release date of May 14. Meanwhile, the Technicolor people, working from the approved final cut, were busy preparing their three-color dye transfer prints, a considerably more complex and time-consuming process than black and white printing or the color processes used subsequently in the last twenty-seven years.

The Reviews

In early April, *The Adventures of Robin Hood* was sneak previewed—with Korngold's music—in Pomona, near Los Angeles. In a telegram to executives in Warners' New York office, Jack Warner said, "In history of our company never have we had picture that scored in front of audience like this did." On April 11, Hal Wallis wired New York: "Had second sneak preview Warner Bros. Downtown theater [in Los Angeles] and went even better than Pomona, which is hard to believe." Two weeks later there was a preview at Warners' Hollywood theater. Wallis cabled that the screening was "absolutely sensational. Spontaneous applause throughout picture. Terrific hand at finish. Review sensational. Important people throughout business phoning congratulations this morning. . . . Its success is without question." Few or no changes were made to the film after the previews, according to available evidence.

The picture opened to outstanding critical and audience plau-
dits. Almost all the reviews praised the film as superlative entertainment. Frank S. Nugent in the *New York Times* (May 13, 1938)
said that "life and the movies have their compensations and
such a film as *The Adventures of Robin Hood* . . . is payment in
full for many dull hours of picture-going. A richly produced,
bravely bedecked, romantic and colorful show, it leaps boldly to
the forefront of this year's best and can be calculated to rejoice
the eights, rejuvenate the eighties and delight those in between." Howard Barnes in the *New York Herald Tribune* (May 13,
1938) commented: "There is a great deal of fabulous make-be-
lieve in the film, but it holds its own as entertainment in any
coin of the realm." *Variety* (April 27, 1938) stated that "it is cine-
matic pageantry at its best. . . . Film is done in the grand manner of silent day spectacles with sweep and breadth of action. . . .
Superlative on the production side." *The Commonweal* (May 27,
1938): "[It] is beautifully done in Technicolor without its looking
like an overpainted postcard." *Cue* (May 14, 1938): "A brilliant
Technicolor production, scintillating with the technical perfection we have come to expect from Warner Studios." Mark Van
Doren in *The Nation* (June 4, 1938) was not so enthusiastic:
"Warner Bros. have put everything into *The Adventures of Robin
Hood* that was necessary, and a few more things for good luck. . . .
To my taste, however, it has been overpolished, and it is too
clean. Hollywood can learn something from Europe about the
convincingness of a little disarray, a little honest disorder. . . .
But the film is better than I have said. It is really charming." The
only truly negative review I have been able to discover was written by C. A. Lejeune for the London *Observer*. Not at all typical
of the British reaction to the film, this critic said in part: "It must
have been an almost superhuman task to make a dull film on the
subject of Robin Hood, but the Warner Brothers, who have never
flinched from major difficulties, have almost managed it. I don't
know when I have seen more money, more care, and more important workmanship lavished on such a stupendous presenta-
tion of the obvious."[17]

17. C. A. Lejeune, *Chestnuts in Her Lap* (London: Phoenix House, 1947), p. 41.

The Elements of Success

Since timing dictates the shaping of so many things, there is no question that Warner Brothers in 1937–38 was particularly suited to make this film. The studio had been drenched in the populist tradition with its dramas and melodramas of injustice and social protest: *I Am a Fugitive from a Chain Gang* (1932), a contemporary study of injustice; *Voltaire* (1933), wherein that philosopher is depicted as the champion of the downtrodden people of eighteenth-century France, inflaming the subjects to rebellion; *Captain Blood*, the precursor to *Robin Hood* with its justified revolt against authority and numerous other parallels; *The Life of Emile Zola*, highlighting the author–social reformer's fight against tyranny and injustice. Also, Warners had become the large-scale action specialists of the major studios (for example, *The Charge of the Light Brigade*).

Then there was Curtiz—this vigorous and imaginative director had found a perfect home at Warners in the thirties and forties. His fluid use of the camera, dynamic composition, expressionistic overtones (figure 22), and flair for staging action sequences[18] were all in keeping with this kind of vehicle (although he was quite versatile, excelling in almost every genre). His drive and ruthless passion for film were considerably beyond most of his contemporaries. Curtiz's first day's work on *Robin Hood*, after he took over from Keighley, began with the establishing shots of the Great Hall in Nottingham Castle during the banquet of the Norman barons. This entire sequence, including Robin's escape, is vivid testimony to his prowess and instinctive dramatic sense. He was a director-collaborator who

---

18. Despite some opinions to the contrary, Curtiz definitely was the director of most of the action scenes in the big pictures he did. For example, he staged all of the action scenes in *Captain Blood* and *The Sea Hawk* (other than miniature work), almost everything in *Dodge City*—including the marathon saloon brawl—and all of *The Charge of the Light Brigade*, with the exception of some shots of the leopard hunt without principal players, which B. Reeves Eason handled, and the charge itself, for which Curtiz served as co-director with Eason. (Eason was also the sole director of some second-unit shots for the charge.) The evidence is available in the production memos and the daily production reports, which include specific details as to who did what on any given day, and where, during filming.

enhanced scripts and breathed life into them in an exuberant manner. Jack Warner and, more directly, Hal Wallis, since that was his function, were fine complements. Their policies, script-editing expertise, production checks and balances, and shrewd editorial judgment were what made Warner Brothers function extremely well at that time.

Another important element in this unique mesh—besides the Technicolor process—was the excellent casting, including Errol Flynn who, at twenty-nine, was at his peak and perfect for the role, with just enough seasoning. He was "hero" personified and Olivia his by now ideal screen lover. With this chemistry, their romantic scenes, especially, in this picture were played with believable ardor, grace, and more than a touch of humor (figure 12).

Korngold's score was a splendid added dimension. His style for the Flynn swashbucklers resembled that of the creators of late nineteenth-century and early twentieth-century German symphonic tone poems. It incorporated chromatic harmonies, lush instrumental effects, passionate climaxes—all performed in a generally romantic manner. Korngold's original and distinctive style was influenced by the Wagnerian leitmotiv, the orchestral virtuosity of Richard Strauss, the delicacy and broad melodic sweep of Puccini, and the long-line development of Gustav Mahler. The "Robin of Locksley" theme, along with its expansion and development, is the only material in the *Robin Hood* score that Korngold did not write specifically for this film. Composed in 1919 as a symphonic overture, *Sursum Corda*, it proved effective underneath the lengthy sequence of Robin's escape from Nottingham Castle.

Audiences then and now loved the movie, many people going back to see it time and again. During World War II, it was one of the most popular films shown to members of the armed forces overseas on bases or on ships. In 1948, ten years after its first release, Warners reissued the film everywhere with new Technicolor prints, treating it in the manner of one of their big, fresh attractions. The public flocked once again, the picture performing better than most new films at the box office and certainly better than the usual revival of an old movie. It was reissued another time—but in black and white only and on a more limited basis—just before being sold to television in the mid 1950s, where it has been a perennial favorite. In a poll taken in 1977 by Joe Walders for *TV Guide*, program directors of television stations throughout the country were asked to name the ten most popular, most often shown movies in their markets. *Robin Hood* was number five, preceded by—in order of popularity—*Casablanca*, *King Kong*, *The Magnificent Seven*, and *The Maltese Falcon*.

The Adventures of Robin Hood avoided the pitfalls that plague so many other films in the historical romance genre. The subject had been extraordinarily popular for over six hundred years, and Warner Brothers had the good sense not to drastically alter the material or to make it seem considerably more than it was. All the elements were handled in a relatively simple and straightforward manner. The dialogue was not too flowery and archaic in an attempt to be faithful to the period; vigor and pace always offset the pomp and ceremony, and nothing tedious marred the proceedings. Rather than lasting two hours or longer, as so many costume adventure films do, *Robin Hood* runs its course in a brisk one hour and forty-two minutes. During that time, the film is literally crammed with incident and action—all of it pointed and interestingly staged. There is a prevailing humor, not forced or awkward, but light-hearted, impudent, and indigenous.

Relatively little about the picture dates, except in a charming way. The characters, costumes, castle, and forest are idealized, but then the film is not a document of medieval life; rather, it is a fairy tale illustrated by Technicolor. The "love interest," usually clumsy and arbitrary in costume adventure films, is here properly motivated and nicely woven into the plot fabric. And the rich score serves as marvelous connective tissue, literally sweeping the film along.

Many other productions of the Robin Hood legend followed. Some, like Disney's live-action feature of 1952, *The Story of Robin Hood*, presented a substantially similar story with variations in the details. Several offered further adventures of the outlaw that were but figments in the minds of screenwriters. Finally, there were various tales relating to a son and even a daughter of

Robin Hood, none of which had any basis whatsoever in the evolution of the legend.

In 1955 the first of approximately 150 half-hour episodes made in England and dealing with the legend was introduced on television with Richard Greene as the outlaw. Disney even did an animated feature film version in the 1970s, and the BBC produced twelve half-hour programs called *The Legend of Robin Hood* in 1975, which have particular merit due to the high quality in all aspects of the approach and execution.

But just as the Fairbanks production was everybody's favorite in the 1920s, the definitive Robin Hood for most people since 1938 is the Warners version, wherein many elements of popular entertainment are beautifully fused: fairy tale romance, spectacle, color, action, pageantry, humor, the triumph of right over might, the exultation of the Free Spirit, the charm of the greenwood, and a vague nostalgia for a partly mythical age of chivalry.

REFERENCES

In addition to the abundant materials from the Warner Film Library (see Inventory) and the individuals and research centers named in the Acknowledgments, the following written works were important in the preparation of this volume:

Books

Appleby, John T. *England Without Richard: 1189–1199*. London: G. Bell and Sons, 1965.

Appleby, John T. *John, King of England*. New York: Alfred A. Knopf, 1959.

Dobson, R. B., and Taylor, J. *Rymes of Robyn Hood: An Introduction to the English Outlaw*. Pittsburgh: University of Pittsburgh Press, 1976.

Heal, Edith. *Robin Hood*. New York: Rand McNally, 1928.

Lloyd, Alan. *The Maligned Monarch: A Life of King John of England*. Garden City: Doubleday, 1972.

Munday, Anthony. *The Death of Robert, Earl of Huntingdon*. 1601. Malone Society Reprint. Oxford: University Press, 1967.

————. *The Downfall of Robert, Earl of Huntingdon*. 1601. Malone Society Reprint. Oxford: University Press, 1965.

Newbolt, Henry, ed. *The Greenwood: A Collection of Literary Readings Relating to Robin Hood*. London and Edinburgh: Thomas Nelson and Sons, 1925.

Noyes, Alfred. *Sherwood; or, Robin Hood and the Three Kings*. New York: Frederick A. Stokes Company, 1911. A play in five acts.

Peacock, Thomas Love. *Maid Marian*. London: Macmillan, 1959. Originally published in 1822.

Pyle, Howard. *The Merry Adventures of Robin Hood of Great Renown in Nottinghamshire*. New York: Charles Scribner's Sons, 1883.

Richards, Jeffrey. *Swordsmen of the Screen: From Douglas Fairbanks to Michael York*. London: Routledge and Kegan Paul, 1977.

Ritson, Joseph, ed. *Robin Hood: A Collection of Poems, Songs, and Ballads*. London: George Routledge and Sons, 1884. Originally published in 1795.

Scott, Sir Walter. *Ivanhoe*. London: Adam and Charles Black, 1893. Originally published in 1819.

Smith, Harry B., and deKoven, Reginald. *Robin Hood*. Chicago: Slason Thompson and Co., 1890. A comic opera.

Periodical

"Warner Brothers," *Fortune*, December 1937, pp. 110 ff.

Unpublished Materials

Burbank and Culver City, Calif. Warner Bros. and MGM. Early script versions, by Bernard McConville and Philip Dunne, originally written for Reliance Pictures.

Sigman, Paula M. "Robin Hood for the Twentieth Century Child." Master's thesis, University of California at Los Angeles, 1975.

1. *The special Warner Brothers logo designed for this film to precede the main title.*

2. *Main title.*

42

3. *Sir Robin of Locksley entering Nottingham Castle for the Norman banquet.*

4. *The meeting of Robin and Little John (from the old ballads).*

5. *Robin forces Friar Tuck to carry him across the stream (from the old ballads).*

6. *Robin and Friar Tuck duel in the stream (modified from the old ballads).*

7. Left to right: The sheriff of Nottingham, Lady Marian, and Sir Guy of Gisbourne leading the treasure caravan.

8. Robin about to swing across the road on a vine-covered rope to greet Sir Guy's party.

45

9. *The archery tournament (from the old ballads and Sir Walter Scott's* Ivanhoe*).*

10. *Robin, in disguise, on the verge of splitting his opponent's arrow at the archery tournament (from the old ballads and* Ivanhoe*).*

11. *Robin being condemned to the gallows following his capture at the archery tournament.*

12. *Robin and Marian in her castle chamber.*

13. *Lady Marian overhears the plan to murder King Richard. Left to right: Prince John, Sir Guy, Dickon Malbete, and the Bishop of the Black Canons.*

14. *King Richard and his retinue, disguised as monks, meet Robin and his band in Sherwood (from the old ballads).*

15. *King Richard challenging Friar Tuck in sport. (Still photo. This scene was deleted in the editing room.)*

16. *Marian imprisoned for treason in the castle dungeon.*

17. *The coronation procession. Almost all of Nottingham Castle shown in this scene is a matte painting.*

18. *Still photo showing the full-scale but fragmentary castle structure before the matte painting was added.*

19. *The coronation procession.*

20. *The Bishop of the Black Canons at the coronation.*

21. *The battle royal between Robin and his men and Sir Guy's and Prince John's forces.*

22. *The climactic duel between Robin and Sir Guy embellished with director Michael Curtiz's expressionistic effects.*

23. *Errol Flynn and Basil Rathbone do their own dueling with broadswords.*

24. *"Arise, Robin, baron of Locksley, earl of Sherwood and Nottingham, and lord of all the lands and manors appertaining thereto . . . ".*

The Adventures of Robin Hood

Screenplay
by
NORMAN REILLY RAINE
and
SETON I. MILLER

The Adventures of Robin Hood

FADE IN

1.   FLUTTERING BANNER   DAY

containing the brilliantly colored royal arms of Richard, the Lion-Heart, king of England. SUPERIMPOSED on this are the following titles:

> In the year of Our Lord 1191, when Richard, the Lion-Heart, set forth to drive the infidels from the Holy Land, he gave the regency of his kingdom to his trusted friend, Longchamp, instead of to his treacherous brother, Prince John.

DISSOLVE TO:

> Bitterly resentful, John hoped for some disaster to befall Richard, so that he, with the help of the Norman barons, might seize the throne for himself. And then on a luckless day for the Saxons . . . [1]

DISSOLVE TO:

2.   SMALL SQUARE   TOWARD CORNER

A sizable crowd has gathered, and people are streaming in from all directions. The scene is lighted by several flaring, flickering torches. The drum men are still rolling the drums. A crier is standing above the crowd, shouting the news as we come to scene.

CRIER:

> News has come from Vienna! King[2] Leopold of Austria has seized King Richard on his return from the Crusades. Our king is being held prisoner.

3. MED. SHOT   CROWD
As the crier continues, we see the terrifying effect of the news on the faces in foreground. A growing babel mingles with the rolling of drums and the shouting of the crier as he finishes his pronouncement and starts repeating it for newcomers.

CRIER (continuing):
Nothing further is known. His Highness Prince John will make further public pronouncement tomorrow!

DISSOLVE TO:

4. INT. CASTLE   PRINCE JOHN'S STUDY   AT WINDOW
CLOSE TRUCK SHOT
Prince John is standing motionlessly, looking out and down through window, a gleam of cruel triumph in his eyes. From off scene comes the distant sound of the rolling of drums, the babel of the crowd, and over it the distant voice of the announcer, repeating the news.

CAMERA TRUCKS SLOWLY BACK, revealing Sir Guy standing a short distance away, a grim smile of pleasure on his face. There is a moment's silence. Prince John continues to watch out the window as he speaks.

PRINCE JOHN:
How are the dear Saxons taking the news?

SIR GUY (a sardonic smile):
They're even more worried than Longchamp, Your Highness.

PRINCE JOHN:
They'll be more than worried when I get through squeezing the fat out of their pampered hides.

SIR GUY (at once alert):
You're going to act on your plans?

Prince John turns to Sir Guy with a growing ironic chuckle.

PRINCE JOHN:

> What better moment than this, my friend? Who would have thought my brother would be considerate as to get himself captured and leave all England to my tender care?

SIR GUY (the sardonic smile is broader):
> He may disapprove when he returns.

PRINCE JOHN:

> *If* he returns . . . and I'll see to it that he doesn't. (He laughs aloud.)

As he continues, he crosses the room toward a table with food and wine on it, and Sir Guy accompanies him. They talk as they cross.

PRINCE JOHN (continuing):
> We must drink to this moment, Sir Guy . . . Golden days are ahead!

5. MED. CLOSE SHOT   AT TABLE

Prince John quickly picks up a container of red wine, filling two goblets sitting near the edge of the table.

PRINCE JOHN (chuckling):
> I'll assign tax districts to you tomorrow.

Sir Guy picks up his goblet quickly, lifting it in a triumphant toast.

SIR GUY:
> Tomorrow!

As Prince John puts down the wine jug and starts to pick up his own goblet, he knocks it over. The wine spills toward the edge of the table and runs over the edge, falling to the stone floor in a small trickling stream.

As the goblet topples over, CAMERA TRUCKS SWIFTLY into a CLOSE SHOT of it and PANS DOWN to the wine dripping on the floor. And we

DISSOLVE TO:

6. WATERING TROUGH   TRUCK SHOT
We discover CLOSE-UP of rough flagstones and a fallen sword with blood dripping slowly down on them. TRUCK BACK to reveal a Saxon farmer lying half across a rough wood or stone watering trough with an arrow in his back, while in background four or five Norman horsemen are swiftly rounding up about twelve fine horses, bringing some out of the small barn, and herding them away.[3]

FAST DISSOLVE TO:

7. MED. CLOSE SHOT   BLACKSMITH'S FORGE   NIGHT
Several Norman men-at-arms hold a Saxon prisoner—a man better dressed than a serf. A soldier is hammering an iron collar and leg manacles, connected by chains, onto the man. A mild little priest puts a protesting hand on the soldier's arm.

PRIEST:
This man is freeborn. A landowner! You can't make a slave of him!

MAN-AT-ARMS:
Didn't he refuse to send his men to work in Guy of Gisbourne's fields?

PRIEST:
But—

Another soldier whirls the priest around and strikes him brutally to the ground.

DISSOLVE TO:

8. EXT. BUTCHER SHOP   NOTTINGHAM   DAY
MED. CLOSE SHOT
A number of Norman soldiers are carrying out a side of beef and three dressed mutton. The proprietor follows them out, almost tearfully protesting.

BUTCHER:
But who's to pay me?

SOLDIER (indignantly):
> Pay! Pay! That's all you Saxons think of! Didn't I tell you this was for Prince John, who's just come up from London?

As he shoves the butcher roughly aside and the hostile crowd that has gathered murmurs resentfully,

DISSOLVE TO:

9. FULL SHOT   SHERWOOD FOREST   DAY
Sir Guy of Gisbourne, with other knights in armor, their squires, and an escort of mounted men under an under-officer, Dickon Malbete, is riding along a road in Sherwood Forest. As they pass, CAMERA PANNING with them.

10. MED. SHOT   GLADE IN SHERWOOD FOREST   DAY
A deer is grazing.

11. CLOSE SHOT   TREE AND UNDERGROWTH
SHOOTING toward the deer.

CAMERA PANS UP TO:

12. MED. SHOT   MUCH-THE-MILLER'S-SON
lying out on a branch, looking toward the deer, and drawing an arrow to his bow. His face is round, snub-nosed, with a certain furtive humor. He is dressed in a sleeveless leather jerkin and close-fitting leather breeches that come to his knees. His hair is wild and matted, his whole person uncouth. He is barefoot. As he looses the arrow, then drops agilely to the ground,

13. INTERCUT   Introduction Robin Hood and Will of Gamwell, both ride in spectacularly taking an obstacle, then all of a sudden stop and see:

14. CLOSE SHOT   THE DEER
on the ground, impaled by the arrow. Much runs quickly into the scene and kneels beside the deer. Looking about with quick stealth, he draws a knife, about to draw the

animal. Then he halts suddenly, and his head jerks up. He listens intently.

15.   MED. CLOSE SHOT   SIR GUY AND SQUIRE
looking idly off into the forest as they ride along. Suddenly Sir Guy's attention focuses. He halts. Then, with furious face, and gesturing his immediate bodyguard to follow him, he spurs his horse abruptly from the road into the forest, toward Much. The balance of the procession halts.

16.   MED. SHOT   THE GLADE
As Much commences to run, the Norman horsemen thunder down on him. He dodges, knife in hand, but two horsemen, one of them Dickon, hurl themselves on him from their horses at full gallop and bear him to the ground.

CUT TO:

17.   MED. CLOSE SHOT   MUCH AND SIR GUY
as the soldiers jerk Much to his feet, fighting madly, and drag him forward to the knight. One or two others dismount to help subdue him. He is held, panting, frothing with desperation and rage, by Dickon and others.

SIR GUY:
Your name, you Saxon dog . . .

MUCH (savage):
A better one than yours!

DICKON (smashes him on the mouth):
Mind your manners! This is Sir Guy of Gisbourne.

MUCH:
Sir Guy or the devil—there's little to choose between 'em!

He is silenced by brutal kicks and blows. A man-at-arms holds a knife point at his throat.

DICKON:
>   What are you called?

MUCH (sullen):
>   Much-the-Miller's-Son.

SIR GUY:
>   You know it's death to kill the king's deer?

MUCH (desperate defiance):
>   And death from hunger if I don't! Thanks to you and the rest of Prince John's Norman cutthroats at Nottingham Castle!

DICKON:
>   Shut up, you—!

MUCH (to Dickon):
>   I'll not shut up for any Norman hedge-robber! (To Sir Guy.) Kill me if you like, but I'll have my say first! You can beat and starve and rob us Saxons now! But when King Richard escapes . . .

>   CUT TO:

18.   CLOSE SHOT   SIR GUY
as he listens, with angry face.

MUCH'S VOICE:
>   'E'll take ye by the scuff of your necks and fling you into the sea!

Sir Guy, in overpowering fury, snatches out his sword and raises it, about to cut Much down, when a great black war arrow screams out of the forest, strikes the broadsword from his hand, and hurls it a dozen yards away. Sir Guy, with an exclamation, echoed in awe by his men, grasps his stinging wrist with the other hand.

>   CUT TO:

19.   MED. CLOSE SHOT   THE GROUP
as they turn and stare off.

>   CUT TO:

20.   MED. CLOSE SHOT   ROBIN AND WILL   DAY
Robin and Will are sitting mounted, on the rim of the
glade, watching. Robin hands his bow to Will and both
ride forward.

CUT TO:

21.   MED. SHOT   SIR GUY AND GROUP
as Robin and Will ride up. Robin is dressed in a hunting
dress of Lincoln green. Will is in bright scarlet and carries, slung over his shoulder, a small mandolinlike instrument. Sir Guy glares at Robin who looks sardonically
amused.

SIR GUY:
What the devil—

ROBIN (interrupts, ironically amused):
Come now, Sir Guy—you wouldn't kill a man for
telling the truth!

SIR GUY:
If it amused me!

ROBIN:
You can be thankful *my* humor's of different sort.

One of Sir Guy's men has retrieved the sword and hands
it to him. Sir Guy sheathes it with a scowl.

CUT TO:

22.   MED. CLOSE SHOT   THE GROUP
from a different angle.

SIR GUY:
By what right do you interfere with the king's
justice?

ROBIN:
By a better right than you have to misuse it. And
that goes for your master, Prince John, too!

SIR GUY:

> I'll give him that message at the barons' meeting in Nottingham tonight.

ROBIN:

> Ah, yes . . . the barons' meeting! Perhaps I'll tell him in person.

SIR GUY:

> This is a Norman meeting—

ROBIN (reassurance):

> Now, now . . . don't apologize. My nose isn't that sensitive . . . (Kindly.) I'll pretend not to notice them. (Ignores Sir Guy's fury.) Besides, Prince John needs talking to. He's getting a bit out of hand. (Nods.) That's a very good idea! Tell him I'll be there.

SIR GUY:

> Even your insolence wouldn't dare that!

WILL (languid contempt):

> Would you lay a wager . . . ?

Sir Guy flashes him an angry glance, then turns to Dickon and indicates Much.

SIR GUY:

> Fetch him along!

Robin rides between Dickon and Much, brushing Dickon none too gently aside.

ROBIN:

> But why? What's he done?

SIR GUY:

> He's killed a royal deer.

ROBIN (cheerfully):

> You're wrong—as usual. (Pause.) *I* killed that deer.

SIR GUY (incredulous):

> *You?*

ROBIN (coolly):
> From the wood yonder. (Gestures to the distant edge
> of the wood.) This fellow's only my servant.

Sir Guy stares in disbelief. His squire spurs forward. As
he does, Much slips away a little distance and stands
watching.

SIR GUY'S SQUIRE:
> That's impossible, Sir Guy! It's a good hundred
> paces. There's not a bowman living, could—

SIR GUY:
> You're right!

CUT TO:

23.   TWO SHOT   ROBIN AND SIR GUY

ROBIN (smiles):
> Is he? I tickled your wrist at the same distance. And
> now, if you'll excuse me . . .

He gestures to Much to leave, and Much moves a few
paces off.

SIR GUY:
> For killing the king's deer, the penalty is death,
> whether for serf or noble—

Robin, as though absentminded, reaches across and takes
his bow from Will, fits another arrow to it, and lets it
point straight at Sir Guy's heart.

ROBIN (innocently):
> Even if I intended the meat for Prince John's own
> table?

24.   MED. SHOT   THE GROUP
Sir Guy looks at the arrow, then hard at Robin, who
smiles. Will of Gamwell unslings from his shoulder a
small mandolinlike instrument and looks impudently at
Sir Guy. The latter wheels his horse and starts to leave

the glade. As he does, Will of Gamwell idly strums his instrument and murmurs a song just loud enough to carry to Sir Guy's ears, his eyes roving toward him in pretended innocence.

WILL OF GAMWELL (singing):
> There was a knight,
> Who stormed a hill
> With full ten thousand men;
> And when, at last,
> The top was won
> He tumbled down again.[4]

Sir Guy, close-lipped, but with a murderous look, passes on, followed by his men.

25. MED. CLOSE SHOT   ROBIN
as he looks after them. [Much] approaches, grasps Robin's hands in both of his, and places them on his head in token of fealty.

MUCH (humble gratitude):
> Thanks, good master . . .

ROBIN:
> Look before you shoot, next time, little man.

MUCH (humbly):
> From this day, master, I foller only you.

ROBIN:
> Me? Why you don't even know me!

MUCH:
> Don't know yer? Tck-tck! (Wags his head.) Why, bless yer 'eart, there ain't a poor Saxon in all Nottinghamshire as doesn't know and pray for Sir Robin of Locksley! Take me for yer servant—

ROBIN:
> But I don't need—

MUCH:
> In the 'ole forest there's no such 'unter as me. I'll be faithful—

ROBIN:
> But I tell you, I've no need—

MUCH:
> I ask no pay. Only to foller you—

ROBIN:
> But—

MUCH (obstinate):
> Where you goes, I'll foller!

Robin stares at him in anger for a moment; then, yielding to the doglike devotion in Much's eyes, he pats his shoulder in assent.

ROBIN (smiles):
> Fetch the deer, then.

As Much runs out of scene, Robin and Will ride on at a walk, CAMERA PANNING with them. Much returns into the shot following them, the carcass of the deer on his shoulders.

DISSOLVE TO:

26.   TITLE:
> The great cold hall of Nottingham Castle, the stronghold of Sir Guy of Gisbourne, knew an unaccustomed warmth this night, for Prince John and his friends were met to celebrate a promising future.

DISSOLVE TO:

27.   FULL SHOT   GREAT HALL OF NOTTINGHAM CASTLE   NIGHT
illuminated by torches in iron cressets. On the walls are the colorful banners of Norman knights, each with its heraldic device of lions or leopards, rampant or couchant, boars, unicorns, etc., in brilliant hues. A table is

set for supper, which is being served by liveried ser-
vants of Sir Guy of Gisbourne. Present are Sir Guy,
Prince John, Lady Marian, the high sheriff of Not-
tingham, the Bishop of the Black Canons, Sir Ivor le
Noir, Sir Geoffrey le Grimme, Sir Nigel de Crecy, Sir
Mortimer of Leeds, Sir Ralf of Durham, Sir Baldwin de
Mortain, Sir Norbert de Bayeux, and Sir Boron de
Rochepot, as well as other Norman knights and ladies.
Behind each knight stands his squire. Great boar hounds
roam the hall, snapping up bits of meat thrown to them
from the table. There may or may not be minstrel music.

CAMERA MOVES UP TO:

28.   MED. CLOSE SHOT   PRINCE JOHN AND IMMEDIATE GROUP
Prince John's group consists of Lady Marian, Sir Guy,
the Black Bishop, the high sheriff, Sir Ivor, and other
knights. They are eating and talking, all in great good
humor. Prince John eats no meat and drinks no wine,
but is resplendently dressed and bejeweled.

PRINCE JOHN (to Marian, jovially):
   This is what I like! Good food . . . good company
   . . . (pinches her cheek) and a beautiful woman to
   flatter me! (Beams around him.) Wasn't it worth
   coming from London with me, to see what stout fellows our Nottingham friends are? Take Sir Guy of
   Gisbourne, now—

MARIAN:
   Must I take him, Your Highness?

PRINCE JOHN:
   Why—you like him, don't you?

MARIAN:
   We-ell . . . he's a Norman, of course—

PRINCE JOHN:
   Is that the only reason you like him?

MARIAN (quietly):
Isn't that reason enough for a royal ward, who must obey her guardian?

PRINCE JOHN:
Nay—I'd not force you, my lady . . .

29.   TWO SHOT   MARIAN AND PRINCE JOHN
as he leans closer, serious.

PRINCE JOHN:
. . . but he's our most powerful friend in these shires. He's already in love with you . . . and if I could promise him marriage to a royal ward . . . (he looks at her; she is silent) it would help my plans—

MARIAN:
Perhaps when I know him better—

PRINCE JOHN:
Of course! You're a sensible girl . . . (Looks about him, to Sir Geoffrey.) Any more Saxon objections to our new tax?

30.   MED. CLOSE SHOT   PRINCE JOHN AND GROUP

SIR GEOFFREY:
Objections, Your Highness . . . ? With a Saxon dangling from every gallows tree between here and Charnwood?

This brings a roar of laughter.

PRINCE JOHN:
Well said, Sir Knight! (To Sir Guy, wagging a playful finger.) But not too many, mind—or we'll have nobody left to till our land and pay their taxes.

There is another burst of laughter.

31.   CLOSE SHOT   SIR GUY
as he frowns in unpleasant recollection.

SIR GUY:
> There's one, I'd except, Your Highness—a certain Saxon . . .

PRINCE JOHN'S VOICE:
> Who's that?

SIR GUY:
> Sir Robin of Locksley!

32.   MED. CLOSE SHOT   PRINCE JOHN AND GROUP
Prince John stares at Sir Guy, astonished at his venom.

PRINCE JOHN:
> What's he been doing?

SIR GUY:
> Nothing less than killing a royal deer in Sherwood Forest today.

PRINCE JOHN (instantly irate):
> And didn't you take him?

SIR GUY:
> I must admit, that would have been something of a problem.

LADY MARIAN (curiously):
> A *Saxon*, a problem?

SIR IVOR:
> He's a notorious troublemaker, my lady!

SIR GEOFFREY:
> Aye—an impudent, reckless rogue who goes about the shire stirring up the Saxons against authority!

PRINCE JOHN:
> You mean—he defies *me*?

BLACK BISHOP (unctuously):
> Not only defies Your Highness, but has the insolence to set himself up as a protector of the people.

HIGH SHERIFF (importantly):
 I'd have captured him long ago, but . . .

He hesitates, uncertain.

PRINCE JOHN (angrily impatient):
 But what—?

HIGH SHERIFF (lamely):
 Well . . . he's the deadliest archer in England, and—

PRINCE JOHN (contemptuously):
 —and you're afraid of him! (Raging, to Sir Guy.) I
 want him taken and hanged! At once—d'ye hear?
 I'll not tolerate—

He stops suddenly. SOUND TRACK carries the noise of a
hefty scuffle, exclamations, and blows. As the men present, startled, half rise, their hands flying to their sword
hilts,

                          CAMERA DRAWS BACK TO:

33. MED. FULL SHOT   THE GREAT HALL
 SHOOTING toward the door. It bursts open and Robin enters the room, throwing off the lackeys who are trying
 to hold him back. Across his shoulder is the body of the
 deer. Prince John gets to his feet and stares. Robin's assailants withdraw in embarrassment. The castle seneschal, uncertain what to do, hesitates in nervous embarrassment at the door.

PRINCE JOHN (to Sir Guy):
 Who is this—this—

34. CLOSE SHOT   SENESCHAL
 summons courage and does his duty. Announces Robin
 in a loud but shaking voice.

SENESCHAL:
 Sir—Sir Robin of Locksley . . . !

35.　MED. SHOT　ROBIN AND PRINCE JOHN'S GROUP
as Robin strides unconcernedly forward, carrying the
deer. CAMERA PANS with him as he walks to the table and
stops before Prince John.

ROBIN (politely):
　Your Royal Highness . . . ?

Prince John maintains an ominous silence. Robin looks
down the table at the remnants of the meal, then back at
Prince John with an impudent, charming smile.

ROBIN (cheerfully):
　You should really teach Gisbourne hospitality! I no
　sooner enter his castle with a bit of meat—(taps the
　deer; John stares at him) than his starving servants
　try to snatch it from me. (To Sir Guy, mild reproof.)
　You should feed them. They'll work better. (Dumps
　the deer on the table in front of Prince John.) With
　the compliments of your royal brother, King Rich-
　ard, God bless him!

Prince John's anger melts in stupefaction as he stares at
Robin. Then suddenly he throws back his head and
shouts with laughter, sinking back into his chair.

36.　MED. CLOSE SHOT　GROUP OF NORMAN KNIGHTS
They smile wryly, while glaring daggers at Robin. Prince
John's laughter OVER SCENE.

37.　MED. CLOSE SHOT　ROBIN, PRINCE JOHN, MARIAN, AND
GROUP
Prince John wipes tears of mirth from his eyes. Robin
waits, coolly, for him to subside.

PRINCE JOHN (gasps):
　By my faith, you're a bold rascal, Robin—but I like
　you! Have you had meat?

ROBIN (indicates deer):
　None but what I brought, Your Highness.

PRINCE JOHN:
>   Sit down, then! There—opposite me! (Indicates chair already occupied by Sir Ivor.) Get up, Sir Knight, and give him your place.

Sir Ivor, outraged, does not move for a moment. Robin prods him with his thumb, then gestures with it for him to move. Furious, Sir Ivor gets up, and Robin, with a grin, sits down. Servants remove the deer. Robin looks at Sir Guy.

ROBIN (grins):
>   You look very glum, Gisbourne. What's the matter— run out of hangings?

SIR GUY (meaningfully):
>   I know a fit subject for one!

Marian has been staring at Robin through this and looks excessively annoyed that he has taken Sir Ivor's place opposite her. She now rises.

MARIAN (to Prince John, cool disdain):
>   If Your Highness will excuse me—

Prince John detains her, his hand on her arm.

PRINCE JOHN:
>   No—no! Sit down, my dear. He'll not harm you. (To Robin.) This is my ward, the Lady Marian Fitzwalter. I'm leaving her here in Gisbourne's care, while I visit the northern shires.

Robin bows and smiles, but Marian icily ignores him.

38.   THREE SHOT   ROBIN, MARIAN, AND PRINCE JOHN

ROBIN (to Marian):
>   I hope my lady had a pleasant journey from London?

MARIAN (frigid):
>   What you hope can hardly be important.

ROBIN (instantly, to Prince John):
> It's a pity my lady's manners don't match her looks,
> Your Highness.

PRINCE JOHN (looks startled, then gets it and shouts with
laughter):
> Did you hear that, gentlemen? There's poor Gis-
> bourne so much in love with Marian he daren't say
> "boo!" . . . and this saucy fellow gives her better
> than she sends! (Shouts to servants.) Bring him food
> at once! Such impudence must support a mighty
> appetite.

The servants hastily set food before Robin, who falls to.

ROBIN (eating):
> My appetite needs something to support it, for we
> Saxons have little to fatten on when your tax gath-
> erers are through.

39. MED. CLOSE SHOT   PRINCE JOHN AND PARTY

HIGH SHERIFF:
> You think you're overtaxed, eh?

ROBIN (nods energetically):
> Overtaxed, overworked, and paid off with a knife,
> a club, or a rope.

MARIAN (gasps):
> Why—you speak treason!

ROBIN:
> Fluently.

BLACK BISHOP:
> I'd advise you to curb that wagging tongue!

ROBIN:
> A habit I've never formed, Your Grace. (To Prince
> John.) You know, we're not going to put up with
> these oppressions much longer.

He continues cheerfully to eat, helping himself to a draft of ale.

JOHN (swift anger):
Oh—you're not? Then listen to this! (He stands, addresses the room.) As you know, my brother is a prisoner of Leopold of Austria. And I have received a ransom demand of 150,000 gold marks.[5] That means that *you*, my friends, must collect in taxes not two gold marks in the pound but three! (There is a murmur of astonishment. Robin chews slowly, watching Prince John.) And the money's to be turned over to me!

There is dead silence. The knights look at each other.

40.   CLOSE SHOT   ROBIN
He suspends eating.

ROBIN (quietly):
Why to you, Your Highness? King Richard appointed Longchamp as regent.

41.   CLOSE SHOT   PRINCE JOHN
He leans forward, looks up and down the table, his crafty face dark with triumph. Speaks slowly and distinctly.

PRINCE JOHN:
I've kicked Longchamp out! From now on, *I'm* regent of England![6]

42.   FULL SHOT   THE TABLE
There is deathly stillness. Even these Normans, astonished at Prince John's audacity in thus betraying his royal brother, are aghast. Only Sir Guy is undisturbed. He looks secretly jubilant. Prince John gets from his seat and glares up and down the table.

PRINCE JOHN (violent fury):
Confound it—what are you all goggling at? (Hammers the table with a tankard.) Is it so strange that

I decide to rule, when my brother's a prisoner?
(Brutal violence.) And who's to say I shan't? (To Sir
Mortimer, menacingly.) You?

SIR MORTIMER (smooth shrug and smile):
Not I, Your Highness!

PRINCE JOHN (to Sir Geoffrey):
You? (Sir Geoffrey shakes his head. To Sir Ralf.)
You?

SIR RALF:
My sword is yours, Your Highness.

Prince John grunts satisfaction, then he glares in turn at
the high sheriff who is terrified, at the Black Bishop who
is eager to be agreeable, at others, who remain silent and
acquiescent or servilely shake their heads to assure him
they are on his side. Prince John's face clears. He becomes jovial again, sits down, then looks at Robin, who
is slowly chewing.

CAMERA MOVES UP TO:

43.   TWO SHOT   ROBIN AND PRINCE JOHN

PRINCE JOHN (triumphant sarcasm):
And what about my young Saxon cockerel here?

Robin looks him full in the eyes for a moment, still
chewing, but saying nothing. Then with sudden violence he spits the piece of meat he has been eating in
front of Prince John with a grimace of repulsion.

44.   MED. CLOSE SHOT   ROBIN AND PRINCE JOHN
Prince John frowns at this rudeness.

PRINCE JOHN:
What's the matter—have you no stomach for honest
meat?

ROBIN:
For honest meat—yes . . . (rises, says distinctly, with
cool insolence) but I've no stomach for traitors!

77

Prince John half rises, furious.

PRINCE JOHN:
You call *me* traitor?

ROBIN:
You—? Yes. (Looks coolly around at Sir Guy and the Norman knight.) And every man here who gives you allegiance!

Angry Norman voices rise. Prince John motions for silence. Robin continues:

ROBIN:
You've used the king's misfortune to seize his power . . . (gets up from his seat and takes a few steps backward) and you'll use that power with the help (bows to the Norman barons) of your sweet cutthroats here to grind Richard's ransom out of our helpless Saxon hinds—a ransom that will be used not to release Richard but to buy your way to the throne!

A roar of furious protests goes up from the Norman knights.

45.   FULL SHOT   THE TABLE
The knights lean tensely forward, hands on their sword hilts.

SIR GUY (swiftly, to Prince John):
May I—dispose of him, Your Highness?

PRINCE JOHN (face livid with suppressed fury):
No. Let him spout—for the moment. (To Robin, grimly.) And what do *you* propose to do?

46.   CLOSE SHOT   MARIAN
as she tensely watches Robin.

ROBIN'S VOICE:
Do? (Every word is cold, deliberate, distinct, and

emotionless.) From this night on, I'll use every means in my power to fight you!

47. MED. CLOSE SHOT   ROBIN, PRINCE JOHN, AND GROUP
as Robin, almost smiling, leans easily toward Prince John, speaking with quiet, deadly emphasis.

ROBIN:
I'll organize revolt . . . ! Exact a death for a death . . . ! And never stop till every Saxon in our shire can stand up to you, free men, and strike a blow for Richard and England!

PRINCE JOHN (bellow of rage):
Take him! Kill him!

A dozen men with drawn swords leap toward Robin, but his blade flashes out and cuts down the nearest, and he starts for the door.

48. FULL SHOT   THE GREAT HALL
As Robin goes for the door, servants, squires, and knights try to bar his path, but he hacks his way through. Servants try to close the door and cut him off, but he beats them down. As he battles at the door,

49. MED. SHOT   CORRIDOR OUTSIDE GREAT HALL   NIGHT
NOTTINGHAM CASTLE
SOUND TRACK carries the noise of conflict, shouts, and clash of steel. Frightened servants and a man-at-arms or two gather and listen, not daring to go in.

NOTE: This fight and Robin Hood's escape from the castle to be worked out in detail later on.

50. MED. CLOSE SHOT   ROBIN
inside the hall, fighting off his attackers. Already three or four of them have been run through, and their fallen bodies obstruct the others.

51.   MED. CLOSE SHOT   OPEN DOORS IN CORRIDOR   NIGHT
OUTSIDE GREAT HALL
as Dickon Malbete approaches, attracted by the row.

DICKON (to the men-at-arms, draws his blade):
    Come on!

The soldiers thrust the servants aside, and as Dickon
goes through the doorway,

52.   MED. CLOSE SHOT   ROBIN
as Dickon and his men burst into the room. Dickon, behind Robin, raises his sword to smite him down.

53.   CLOSE SHOT   MARIAN
As she sees this, her eyes widen in horror. She screams.

54.   MED. CLOSE SHOT   ROBIN FIGHTING
Warned by Marian's scream, he whirls around in time
to see Dickon. He ducks under the sword stroke and,
coming up, catches Dickon in the belly with his shoulder
and with terrific force heaves him full at his foes. Then,
cutting down a man who opposes him, he dashes out
the doorway and turns for a brief second.

55.   MED. LONG SHOT   ROBIN   IN DOORWAY
from Marian's angle. He looks up at her, flashes her a
salute of thanks with his sword, and is gone.

56.   MED. SHOT   CORRIDOR
as Robin runs out and down the hall, his pursuers pour
out of the great hall and after him, past the lens.

57.   MED. SHOT   CASTLE COURTYARD   NIGHT
A number of men-at-arms and castle servants are gathered around a door leading into the castle. Will of Gamwell and Much—Will mounted, Much standing at the
head of Robin's horse—are waiting restlessly in the

courtyard. The door bursts open and Robin runs out. He pulls up and addresses the servants, etc.

ROBIN (peremptory, to men near the door):
>They've got a traitor inside! Quick—hold the door before he gets out!

The men-at-arms hurl themselves at the door and put their combined weight against it. Robin joins Will and Much, leaps into his saddle, and pulls Much up behind him. They gallop out of scene.

58.   MED. CLOSE SHOT   INT. DOOR OF CASTLE   NIGHT
Sir Ivor, Sir Baldwin, men-at-arms, and servants striving to force the door.

SIR BALDWIN (yells to servants, etc.):
>Put your beef into it. Come on—all together, now!

They make a concerted smash at the door. It begins to yield. Others run down the hall and join them.

59.   MED. CLOSE SHOT   COURTYARD DOOR   NIGHT
as the soldiers hold it.

FAT SOLDIER (grunts and groans):
>Hold fast, lads!

ARCHER:
>Hold the rascal in! (The door begins to force them back.) Throw your weight at it!

They grunt and strive, but inexorably the door opens. Suddenly it gives altogether, and Sir Ivor, Sir Baldwin, and the others burst out.

SIR IVOR:
>You fools! Which way did they go?

A cowed man-at-arms points toward the causeway. Sir Ivor strikes him brutally across the face. Then he and Sir Baldwin run across to the remaining horses, CAMERA

81

PANNING with them, leap into the saddle, and, followed by their running men, gallop for the causeway.

60.   TWO SHOT   SIR IVOR AND SIR BALDWIN   NIGHT
NEAR CAUSEWAY PORTCULLIS
as they ride in and pull to a lunging stop, their hard faces illuminated by the lurid orange flare of the torches. They look this way and that. Their running men come up behind them. Sir Ivor suddenly sees Robin in the distance, points off scene.

SIR IVOR:
There he is!

The two men spur their horses to a fast start.

61.   MED. CLOSE SHOT   ROBIN, WILL, AND MUCH   NIGHT
Their horses are moving in the darkness beside the town wall. From off scene comes the clatter of approaching horses. Discovered, they halt. Will hands Robin his bow and quiver. Robin carefully draws an arrow to his bow and aims it at the figures. As he lets go, we hear the terrible, angry hum of the bowstring.

62.   TWO SHOT   SIR IVOR AND SIR BALDWIN
The first arrow strikes Sir Ivor in the chest with terrible force, hurling him from the saddle. Sir Baldwin rears his horse, looking down a second; then, his face convulsed with rage, he spurs his horse foward.

63.   MOVING SHOT   ROBIN, WILL, AND MUCH
Robin pulls his horse again to a stop and with grim swiftness fits another arrow.

64.   MED. CLOSE SHOT   CAUSEWAY
as Sir Baldwin thunders onto it—men-at-arms running some distance behind, trying to keep up.

65.   CLOSE SHOT   ROBIN
as he lets the arrow go. Again the powerful twang of the bow.

66.   MED. CLOSE PAN   MIDDLE OF CAUSEWAY
as the arrow strikes Sir Baldwin, piercing him through the neck, and his hurtling body flies from the saddle into the road.

67.   MED. CLOSE SHOT   INNER END CAUSEWAY PORTCULLIS
As the men-at-arms start onto the causeway, there is the vicious twang of the bow off scene, and one of them drops, pierced with an arrow. The rest break in panic and seek shelter beside the portcullis.

68.   MED. SHOT   ROBIN, WILL, AND MUCH
As they wheel their horses and dash off into the darkness,

DISSOLVE TO:

69.   MED. SHOT   THE CAUSEWAY   NIGHT
A body of mounted men-at-arms led by Dickon gallop across the causeway and, CAMERA PANNING with them, set out in pursuit of Robin and his friends.

DISSOLVE TO:

70.   MED. SHOT   EDGE OF SHERWOOD FOREST   NIGHT
as Robin, Much, and Will ride swiftly into scene and pull to a halt. The three dismount. Robin slaps Will's horse on the flanks and sends it galloping along the road away from the town. Then, on his signal, the others follow him quickly into the shadow of the trees, Robin leading his horse.

71.   MED. CLOSE SHOT   ROBIN AND FRIENDS   NIGHT
SHOOTING PAST them as they stand, hidden in the edge of the forest, silent, listening. Through a break in the trees the road is visible. Dickon and his men-at-arms gallop past, still in pursuit. The three wait till the mounted troops have passed, then Robin turns to Much.

83

ROBIN:

> Find Crippen the Arrow-maker and his friends. Tell them to pass the word to every man who's been beaten or robbed or tortured . . . The Gallows Oak in Sherwood tomorrow—they'll understand.

MUCH:

> Yes, master.

ROBIN:

> Good luck!

Much mounts and, ducking the bushes, rides out to the road. Robin and Will watch him ride off,[7] then they look at each other.

WILL (disgusted):

> Energetic soul, aren't you?

ROBIN (grins):

> Sorry?

WILL (dismal gesture at forest):

> I suppose we sleep tonight amid the beastly fauna and flora . . .

ROBIN (grin widens):

> It's very healthy.

They start walking into the woods, CAMERA TRUCKING with them.

WILL:

> I'd prefer my warm bed at Locksley.

ROBIN:

> And get taken and hanged?

WILL (disconsolately):

> Better death than discomfort.

Robin grins, and they plunge into the depth of the forest.

DISSOLVE TO:

72. MED. SHOT   TRUCK SHOT   NIGHT
INT. OF SMALL ROOM IN NOTTINGHAM CASTLE
A bare, stone-walled room. The bodies of Sir Ivor and
Sir Baldwin, laid out on their backs on trestles, hands
crossed over breasts in medieval fashion. Men-at-arms
stand guard, and rush-wick candles are burning at their
heads and feet. A black-robed friar murmurs prayers, at
one side. Standing near the bodies is Sir Guy.
CAMERA PANS to reveal at the far end of the room a
candle-lit table. Prince John is seated at table, in a fine
rage, writing on a parchment. Sir Guy stands beside
him, looking down grimly. CAMERA MOVES SLOWLY UP
to the table, holding them in a TWO SHOT as John signs
his name.

PRINCE JOHN (seething; finishes and gets up, hands paper to Sir Guy):
    There's a death sentence for your Robin of Locksley!
    Have it proclaimed in every village that he's an out-
    law, and hang anybody that gives him shelter or
    aid!

SIR GUY:
    Yes, sire.

PRINCE JOHN:
    His possessions are forfeit to the Crown. Seize his
    castle and lands . . . everything he owns . . . (He
    gets up and moves toward the door, accompanied
    by Sir Guy, CAMERA TRUCKING with him.) And just
    to let the people know how the wind has changed,
    the sooner you begin collecting the—the—

SIR GUY (smoothly):
    The ransom . . . sire?

PRINCE JOHN:
    Yes—yes—of course! The ransom! But don't forget
    Locksley!

85

SIR GUY:
I'll have him dangling in a week!

FADE OUT

FADE IN

73.   INT. CRIPPEN'S WORKROOM   MED. SHOT
The first light of dawn streaks in the window, revealing
a workroom with bench littered with arrows and parts,
a small forge in which glows a dim red light of coals,
and a candle still burning on the table.
    Crippen, a small, silver-haired old man, and four or
five other men of varying ages are talking with Much.
The faces of two men are badly scarred.

CRIPPEN (smiling, his eyes seeming to look into the past;
to Much):
The Gallows Oak. We've waited a long time for this.

FIRST MAN (thoughtfully):
And suffered longer.

MUCH:
You've heard Robin's orders. Look nippy, now, and
spread the word!

As Much hurriedly leaves, and the men scatter,

DISSOLVE TO:

74.   CROWD   MED. TRUCK SHOT
In background, on steps of building, a Norman officer is
reading a royal decree:

OFFICER:
. . . by royal decree, Robin of Locksley is declared
an outlaw and sentenced to death. Any person sheltering or aiding him will be hanged . . .

As he speaks, we TRUCK with the beggar as he shoves
his way slowly through the crowd, singling out men,
saying to them, one after the other, in a low voice:

BEGGAR:
>   Meet Robin in Sherwood . . . (To second.) At the
>   Gallows Oak . . .

A series of quick DISSOLVES as the word is passed, first
by some of the men we have seen, then strangers as it
spreads. The reaction is always one of eager assent and
the start of quick preparation.

75.   BLACKSMITH   AT HIS FORGE   DAY
One of the men we have seen walks slowly past, speaking in a low voice.

MAN:
>   Robin—! In Sherwood!

The blacksmith straightens, surprised and alert, then
quickly and grimly starts taking off his leather apron.

76.   TAILOR   ON HIS BENCH   DAY

MAN:
>   Robin—! Gallows Oak!

77.   BUTCHER   AT HIS SHOP DOOR

MAN:
>   . . . at the Gallows Oak.

DISSOLVE TO:

78.   CATTLE DRIVER   EDGE OF VILLAGE   DAY
On road, Crippen is jogging along in his cart, leaving
town, and speaks to man as he passes.

CRIPPEN:
>   Robin is in Sherwood.

79.   WOOD CHOPPERS   EDGE OF FOREST

MAN ON HORSEBACK:
>   Gallows Oak—! Robin!

DISSOLVE TO:

80.　CROWD　MED. TRUCK SHOT
In background, on steps of building, a Norman officer is reading a royal decree:

OFFICER:
. . . by royal decree, Robin of Locksley is declared an outlaw and sentenced to death. Any person sheltering or aiding him will be hanged . . .

And at the same time in foreground, we are TRUCKING with a beggar who moves a few feet, singling out two village men, saying in a low voice to each,

BEGGAR:
Robin—! In Sherwood. (To second man.) Gallows Oak.

DISSOLVE TO:

81.　MED. CLOSE TRUCK SHOT　ROBIN AND WILL
as they walk through the wood in morning light, which streams in shafts of brilliant gold through the greenery. The leaves are jeweled and flashing with dew. Will stops and yawns. Robin looks back at him and grins.

WILL (stretches):
A-a-agh! (Looks resentfully at Robin.) I'm *tired!*

ROBIN:
Tired? After a refreshing sleep in the greenwood?

They start walking again, CAMERA TRUCKING with them.

WILL (morosely):
I've pulled seven acorns out of my ribs!

ROBIN:
Nice fresh air . . . !

WILL:
My teeth ache with chattering!

ROBIN:
Nightingales . . . !

WILL:
An owl, hooting in my ears all night!

A wet branch released by Robin slaps Will in the face.

ROBIN:
He was singing you to sleep!

As they walk along, Robin happy, Will plodding sadly along in rear, they come to a stream and the end of a log which bridges it. As Robin tests it with his foot, Will comes up and bumps into him, then stops. As Robin turns with a grin, he sees Will gazing at something beyond him on the log. As Robin turns and follows his glance,

82. MED. SHOT   LITTLE JOHN
from Robin's angle. Little John, a giant of a man in worn yellow jerkin and hose and a scarlet cap with a green feather, and carrying a great quarterstaff, is standing on the opposite end of the bridge, calmly surveying them.

ROBIN:
There's a lusty infant! D'you suppose I can reason him into joining us?

WILL (morosely):
By the look of him, his quarterstaff does his reasoning for him!

ROBIN (regards Little John and grins):
Well—let's see what he's made of.

WILL (shrugs):
I'm glad it's your skull, not mine!

Robin goes out from his end, Little John advances, and there is not room to pass.

83.   MED. SHOT   THE LOG BRIDGE   DAY

as Robin and Little John meet. Will stands on the bank, bored, to watch.

ROBIN:
Give way, little man!

LITTLE JOHN:
Only to a better man than myself . . .

WILL (from the bank):
Let him pass, Robin. It's too warm to brawl with such a windbag!

LITTLE JOHN (great laugh):
When I've brushed off this fly, I'll give you a dusting for good measure!

Robin turns and winks at Will, then turns to Little John again.

ROBIN (fits arrow to bow and aims it):
This fly has got a mighty sting—

LITTLE JOHN:
I've only a staff and you threaten me with a long bow and grey-goose shaft. Are you not man enough . . . ?

ROBIN:
Give me time to get myself a staff.

The giant nods. Robin returns to the bank and, seizing hold of a strong sapling oak, gives a mighty tug when up it comes. With his dagger he lops off the roots and trims it, then advances across to Little John again. Will sits wearily down to watch.

ROBIN:
Ready?

Quick as light Little John's great staff wings down.

84.　TWO SHOT　ROBIN AND LITTLE JOHN
fighting in the middle of the bridge. They feint, strike, parry, get through with occasional blows, but neither will give ground.

85.　CLOSE SHOT　ROBIN
as he ducks a whistling blow. They talk as they fight.

ROBIN (grins):
If it's a lesson you want—(wham) you've come to the right man.

LITTLE JOHN:
Where—(whish) is he?

ROBIN (whack . . . thump!):
Who?

LITTLE JOHN:
This quarterstaff—(smack) master!

ROBIN (a mighty blow):
Here!

LITTLE JOHN (dodges it, aims one back):
There's my compliments to him! (Another.) You know, friend—(another) I should ask payment for what I'm teaching you today!

ROBIN (gets one home to his ribs):
There's something on account!

86.　CLOSE SHOT　LITTLE JOHN
as he staggers from the blow, then, while still striving to keep his footing, returns one that makes Robin see stars.

LITTLE JOHN (grins):
And there's your change!

87.　MED. SHOT　FIGHT ON BRIDGE
Robin and Little John, panting now, but still full of beans. Will, stretched upon the ground and resting on

his elbow, chewing a straw, watches with interest. Little
John launches a hurricane of blows.

ROBIN (grins):
> You'd make a grand windmill, friend!

LITTLE JOHN (to Will):
> Hey there, pretty fellow . . . ! Play me a tune I can
> make this puny rascal dance to!

ROBIN:
> You want a merrier tune? *How's this?*

Robin launches a terrific swipe, but Little John ducks
under it. Robin, starting to overbalance, teeters helplessly and strives desperately for balance.

88.　MED. CLOSE SHOT　ROBIN AND LITTLE JOHN　ON BRIDGE
Little John coolly steps back. Then like a flash his stave
licks forward and catches Robin across the ankles completing his upset, then whirls up and cracks him one on
the skull and sends him into the stream with a mighty
splash. Little John, roaring with laughter, thrusts his
quarterstaff toward Robin, who is spluttering and
threshing in the brook. Robin grasps the staff and is
drawn to the bank as Little John crosses the bridge,
CAMERA PANNING with them. Will, grinning widely, does
not move.

89.　MED. CLOSE SHOT　THE TRIO
as Robin, dripping, emerges from the stream and holds
out his hand to Little John. Then he sits on the bank.

ROBIN:
> Whew! My head hums like a swarm of bees! (He
> looks up.) What's your name, friend?

LITTLE JOHN:
> John Little . . . and what's yours?

ROBIN:
> Robin.

LITTLE JOHN (astonished delight):
    Not Robin of Locksley? (Robin nods.) Then I'm right
    glad I fell in with you.

WILL (grins):
    'Twas he who did the falling in!

LITTLE JOHN (grinning):
    I hope you'll not hold it against me. I'd like to join
    your company.

ROBIN (puts out his hand, which Little John takes):
    If you can hold a breach like you held the bridge,
    you're one of us, and welcome. (Introduces Will.)
    This is Will of Gamwell.

LITTLE JOHN (looks Will over, disparagingly):
    He took good care not to wet his feathers!

WILL (languidly, yawns):
    Just brain over brawn, my friend.

He shakes hands with so steely a grip that Little John, as
they move off together, glances wonderingly from Will
to his own tingling fingers, then back to Will with
dawning respect.

DISSOLVE TO:

90.   FULL SHOT   ROBIN'S CAMP   NIGHT[8]
The glade is crowded with men in a variety of costume—
serfs, villagers, townfolk, etc. A large bonfire is burning. As Robin quickly mounts a low stump in foreground and holds up his hand, the noise dies to silence.
Robin stands for a moment, keenly studying the faces
around him, then speaks, his voice even, purposeful,
and terse.

ROBIN:
    I've called you here as freeborn Englishmen who
    are loyal to our king. While he reigned over us we
    lived in peace. But since John seized the regency,
    Guy of Gisbourne and the rest of his traitors have

murdered and pillaged. We've all suffered from their cruelty . . .

91.   CLOSE SHOT   ONE-EARED MAN
in ragged serf's garb, listening.

ROBIN'S VOICE:
        . . . the ear-loppings, the beatings . . .

92.   CLOSE SHOT   MAN WITH EYE PATCH
as he listens.

ROBIN'S VOICE:
        . . . the deliberate blindings with hot irons.

93.   CLOSE SHOT   MAN WITH SCARRED MOUTH
as he listens, eyes blazing.

ROBIN'S VOICE:
        . . . the tongue slicing . . . the burning of farms and mistreatment of our women . . .

94.   CLOSE SHOT   ROBIN
as he looks around grimly.

ROBIN:
        It's time we stopped them!

95.   MED. TRUCK SHOT   ROBIN AND CROWD
There is a roar of approval. Robin holds up his hand and continues.

ROBIN:
        This forest is wide . . . It can shelter and clothe and feed a band of good swordsmen . . . good archers. If you're willing to fight for our people, I want you! Are you with me?

There is a gigantic shout of assent and approval, and many sword blades glitter as they leap from their sheaths and flash upward in the medieval gesture of allegiance.

ROBIN:

> Kneel! (They kneel.) Take this oath! (He continues solemnly.) Do you, the freemen of the forest, take oath . . . to despoil the rich only to feed the hungry, clothe the naked and shelter the old and sick . . . to protect all women, Norman or Saxon, rich or poor?

OUTLAWS (as one voice):

> We do!

ROBIN:

> Do you solemnly swear to fight unto death the oppressors of the helpless . . . to remain firm in love of free England . . . and loyally to guard her until the return of our sovereign king . . . Richard the Lion-Heart?

OUTLAWS (as one voice):

> We do solemnly swear!

As Robin bows his head and stillness falls over the forest night,

FADE OUT

FADE IN

96. TITLE:

> But Prince John's reign became even more murderous. Terror spread among the helpless Saxons who knew that resistance meant death. Soon death became preferable to oppression and the defiant oath became more than a thing of words.

DISSOLVE TO:

97. MED. SHOT   HILLTOP   SUNSET
showing foot of gallows and the dangling feet and legs (not the body) of a Saxon serf. Grouped around are a number of Norman men-at-arms and a Norman knight, Sir Boron de Rochepot, in full armor, mounted, with his squire nearby. They form a grim, black silhouette against the blood-red sky. Suddenly SOUND TRACK carries the terrible death note of a bowstring, and a black war ar-

row buries itself in Sir Boron's heart. As he crashes from the saddle, and his startled men turn in all directions looking to see the hidden archer,

DISSOLVE TO:

98.   SARACEN'S HEAD TAVERN   NIGHT

It is storming and lightning outside. A candle burns on the table. Humility is putting a log on the fire that burns in the fireplace. The front door bursts open, and a panic-stricken girl, crying with terror, bursts in, a Norman lunging after her, catching her just inside the door, trying to drag her back outside.

GIRL (in terror):
    No . . . no . . .

As Humility drops the log, she breaks away and runs past Humility, the Norman after her.

GIRL (sobbing):
    Father . . . help me . . . keep him away . . .

Humility, infuriated, hurls himself at the Norman. The latter strikes him viciously, hurling him back.

99.   FIREPLACE

as Humility crashes into the fire, unconscious.

100.   MED. CLOSE SHOT   CORNER OF ROOM

As the Norman rushes into scene, the girl, backed in the corner, shrinks down in stark terror. The man seizes her.

101.   TABLE AND WINDOW

A lightning flash outside silhouettes for an instant a dark figure. A black arrow crashes through the glass and cuts the flame off the candle.

102.   MED. CLOSE SHOT   CORNER

Two close lightning flashes reveal the girl standing alone, the man with an arrow in his back toppling to the floor.

DISSOLVE TO:

103.   MED. CLOSE SHOT   CORNER OF COURTYARD   NIGHT
Men-at-arms, by the light of flares in cressets, are cruelly
lashing a serf's naked back. The serf is strung up by the
thumbs. The knight in charge, Sir Norbert de Bayeux,
signals the man with the scourge to cease.

SIR NORBERT (savagely, to serf):
> Now will you pay your taxes? (The serf's head is
> drooping. He does not answer.) Cut him down!

Another Norman cuts the man's thongs above his
thumbs, and the serf drops to the ground, limp. A second man-at-arms bends briefly over him, then
straightens.

MAN-AT-ARMS:
> He'll die if we lash him again, my lord.

SIR NORBERT:
> Die, will he? (Grumbles.) It'd be just like their Saxon
> impudence. They'd do anything to spite us! String
> him up again!

As they drag the serf from the ground and prepare to
trice him up again, the terrible hum of a black war arrow
whips into the scene and strikes Sir Norbert. It knocks
him like a lightning stroke from his saddle. The men,
dropping the senseless serf, stare around wildly. A man
runs swiftly to Sir Norbert and looks at the arrow.

SOLDIER (horror):
> The black arrow!

The men-at-arms scatter and run in all directions. When
the place is clear, three or four of Robin's men in Lincoln
green, under Robin himself, carrying his bow and a
quiver of black arrows, slip into the scene, pick up the
senseless serf, and run off with him. As Robin follows,

                                        DISSOLVE TO:

104.   INT. HALL   NOTTINGHAM CASTLE   MED. SHOT   NIGHT
A fairly large group of knights and the sheriff of Nottingham are with Sir Guy. It is plain that Robin's campaign has gotten under their skins, for they are upset and wrangling heatedly. Sir Guy is pacing up and down in agitation and rage.

SIR GEOFFREY:
> Five of them dead . . . murdered! Sir Ivor, Nigel, Baldwin, Norbert . . .

SIR GUY (snarling):
> You don't have to name them to *me!*

SIR GEOFFREY:
> Our men can't even lay a hot iron to the eyes of a tax dodger without getting a black arrow in the throat! It's an outrage.

SIR MORTIMER:
> He's got to be stopped!

SIR GUY (angrily):
> Have *you* tried to stop him?

SIR MORTIMER:
> Yes . . . but I couldn't find him.

SIR GEOFFREY:
> What chance has anyone finding him? Every woodcutter and villager is his friend . . .

SHERIFF (pompously):
> . . . and every runaway serf and Saxon thief in the shire is joining him. (Spreading his hands helplessly.) I've sent spies into the forest to find his hiding place . . . but he strikes and is away like smoke!

SIR RALF (angrily):
> While you stay safely at home!

105.   MED. CLOSE SHOT   SHERIFF
as he lumbers angrily to his feet.

SHERIFF:

> Do you question my valor? Am I not personally commanding the force that goes with Sir Guy and Lady Marian to Kenworth Castle to guard the tax money he brings back, with my sword and life? (Pounding table.) I hope this murderer *does* come out of his hiding place.

SIR GEOFFREY (ironically):

> You *hope*?

SIR GUY:

> Enough of this wrangling. I'll lay this outlaw by the heels when I get back . . .

He nods to the sheriff to come with him, and the two take a step toward the door when suddenly, almost as a gesture of supreme contempt and defiance, a heavy black arrow crashes through a window and buries itself quivering in the wall, just above and in the midst of the group. As the knights, Sir Guy, and the sheriff glare at it in impotent rage, we

DISSOLVE TO:

106.   CLOSE SHOT   FISHING BOBBIN OR FLOAT   DAY
floating peacefully on the water.

CAMERA PANS UP TO:

107.   MED. CLOSE SHOT   FRIAR TUCK   DAY
asleep on the bank of the stream. His fishing rod is held down by a stone, and close beside him is an enormous, half-consumed meat pie. His back is to a tree, and nearby on the ground is his steel cap. He is fat as a hogshead and wears a broadsword and dagger. He sleeps with asthmatic snores.

108.   MED. SHOT   FOREST PATH
Robin, with Little John and several men, is coming

through the trees. They are all armed with bow, quiver, dagger, and broadsword. Robin comes to an abrupt halt, motioning his men for quiet. Robin listens, then tiptoes forward and peers through some bushes toward Friar Tuck, grinning. His men come up and also look, smiling.

109. MED. CLOSE SHOT   ROBIN AND HIS MEN
as they gaze with interest at Friar Tuck.

ROBIN (murmurs):
Well-well . . . ! A curtal friar! The very man we need. I'll enlist him!

He starts forward, but Little John checks him.

LITTLE JOHN (warningly):
Be careful, Robin! That's the friar of Fountains Abbey. He's noted for—

MUCH (cuts eagerly in):
That's right! (Nudges Little John for silence.) Noted for 'is piety! (Shakes head admiringly.) A humble soul, 'e is . . . with a heart as gentle as a lamb! Be easy with 'im, master.

He winks at the others. Little John looks as though he would like to intervene, but Much motions him to say nothing. The others grin.

ROBIN (starts forward, magnanimously):
I won't hurt him. (Motions them to stay put.) You'd better stay here, lest you frighten him. And don't interfere.

As he goes out of scene, Much turns with suppressed laughter to the others, some of whom are grinning, while others look puzzled.

MUCH (snickers):
Did you 'ear that? "I won't 'urt 'im," says Robin. We mustn't frighten the pore man, 'e says!

LITTLE JOHN (obtuse protest):
But that friar's the most dangerous swordsman in—

MUCH (checks him):
Shh-h! (Looks across hedge, grinning.) Now we'll 'ave some fun!

110. MED. CLOSE SHOT FRIAR TUCK
as Robin comes softly in and picks up the meat pie (or leg of mutton), taking out his knife and starting to eat with relish. Robin notes something off scene.

111. CLOSE SHOT FRIAR TUCK'S FLOAT
bobbing madly up and down in the water.

112. MED. SHOT ROBIN AND FRIAR TUCK
as Robin carefully puts the foot aside and with a cautious glance at Friar Tuck moves to the fishing rod. He takes it up, draws a wriggling fish out of the water, unhooks it, and drops the line into the water again. Then, putting the flopping fish in the friar's lap, he goes back and sits down, continuing to eat.

113. MED. SHOT TOP OF BUSHY HEDGE
Little John, Much, and the others, grinning broadly, watch over the top.

114. CLOSE SHOT FRIAR TUCK
as the flopping fish awakens him. He looks down and his little pig eyes widen.

FRIAR TUCK:
Bless my soul—a miracle!

Robin shouts with laughter, and Friar Tuck turns quickly and sees him. Friar Tuck lumbers angrily to his feet.

115. MED. SHOT FRIAR TUCK AND ROBIN
as Friar Tuck advances on Robin with a black scowl.

FRIAR TUCK:
> Robber! Thief! Give me back my meat pie!

Robin springs to his feet and draws his sword.

116.   MED. CLOSE SHOT   ROBIN AND FRIAR TUCK
Robin presents his sword point to the friar's belly, while continuing to munch the pie with the other hand.

ROBIN:
> Whao-o-o! Not so fast, good father!

FRIAR TUCK:
> If you're a robber you'll get nothin' from me! I'm a curtal friar, and I'm vowed to poverty.

ROBIN (holds up pie, grins):
> If *this* is your poverty, I'd gladly share it with you.

FRIAR TUCK (angrily):
> That's what you are doing. (Pushes forward.) Give me back my—

ROBIN (pushes him back with sword point):
> Not so close, my ponderous friend. (Continues between mouthfuls.) I live in the forest with a few score good fellows who've everything in life save spiritual guidance and no merit but one.

FRIAR TUCK (suspiciously):
> What's that?

ROBIN (casually):
> We're outlaws.

Friar Tuck nods judicious approval. Then as the word penetrates to him, he does a double take.

ROBIN (continues affably):
> And since we're all newborn to the greenwood, we've chosen you to join us and do our christenings.

FRIAR TUCK:

Not I . . . ! (Looks at rapidly disappearing meat pie.) They've probably all got your taking ways.

ROBIN (serenely commanding):

Of course! But you'll love 'em, one and all. Now, let's go! It's getting late! We'll take the shortcut across the stream.

FRIAR TUCK (bellows indignantly):

I'll not! I'm happy here . . .

Robin drives him forward to the riverbank at the sword's point picking up his bow, CAMERA TRUCKING with them and Friar Tuck sputtering ad lib protests. They halt at the stream.

ROBIN:

Now then . . . I don't care to get wet, so take me on your back.

FRIAR TUCK (indignant surprise):

On my . . .

ROBIN:

You *must* learn obedience. (Pricks him.) Come along—bend!

Friar Tuck glares at him. Robin prods him again with the sword, and he reluctantly bends his back. Robin hops merrily on board and the friar steps into the stream, CAMERA MOVING with them.[9]

On the far bank, Robin jumps down and instantly is seized in the friar's iron grip; the friar's dagger is at his throat.

ROBIN (indignant):

Why—what treachery's this? You know a churchman's forbidden to draw blood!

FRIAR TUCK:

> If blood is drawn, the fault—and the blood—will
> be yours! I prefer the other bank, and on your back
> I'll make it! (As Robin moves.) Be still . . . ! or I'll
> slit your gizzard three fingers deep! Come on—
> bend!

Reluctant and raging, Robin obeys. The friar climbs on
his back and he enters the stream, CAMERA MOVING with
them. The friar, grasping Robin by the hair, pulls and
hauls and digs him with imaginary spurs, playing
horsey, yelling "Giddap!" and having a hell of a time.
Robin under his great weight staggers and flounders.

117. MED. CLOSE SHOT   THE OUTLAWS
They want to go to Robin's aid, but Little John, with a
wide grin, holds them back.

118. MED. CLOSE SHOT   ROBIN AND FRIAR TUCK
as Robin, staggering and slipping, reaches the bank.
Then, as the friar gets off, Robin dives for his ankles,
upsetting him; before he can recover, Robin's sword
point is again at his midriff.

ROBIN:

> You see? The game has turned my way again. Come
> on—bend!

Once more Robin climbs on.

119. MED. CLOSE SHOT   THE OUTLAWS
Little John turns to the others with a pleased smirk and
comically uplifted palms, as though to say, "I told you
so!"

120. MED. SHOT   ROBIN AND FRIAR TUCK
SHOOTING from the outlaw's angle, as the friar carries
Robin. This time Robin is enjoying himself, whacking
Friar Tuck across the butt with the flat of his sword and

treating him like a captious steed. But in midstream the friar gives a mighty heave and Robin goes flying over his head into the stream. He manages to retain his sword, but when he does, thigh deep in water, Friar Tuck is waiting for him, sword in hand. Without further words they cross blades.

121. TWO SHOT   ROBIN AND FRIAR TUCK
in a terrific sword fight, midstream. They cut, slice, jab, feint, swing, and guard, without either having the advantage.

ROBIN (gasping):
> Come now, my fat friend—(feints and cuts and is parried) you *see* I'm the better man. Why not give up . . .

Friar Tuck redoubles his attack.

FRIAR TUCK (panting):
> As soon as I've let a little air—(slice, cut, parry) into your bellows—(a mighty slash which Robin parries) you'll whistle a different tune!

As they continue the duel,

DISSOLVE TO:

122. MED. SHOT   LITTLE JOHN AND OUTLAWS   SUNSET
on the bank in full view now. They are weary of watching and waiting, and some lean against trees or on their weapons; others lie on the ground. Little John stands, legs apart, hands on hips, watching the contest. Much sits cross-legged at his feet.

LITTLE JOHN (yawns):
> Will they never be done? They've been at it for three hours now!

MUCH (chuckles):
> If I know that friar, 'e's only just begun![10]

123.   MED. SHOT   ROBIN AND FRIAR TUCK   SUNSET
still fighting feebly, so weary now that they can hardly
lift their swords, yet neither will give in. Suddenly Friar
Tuck slips backward, trips, and sits down in the water.
Robin, springing forward, helps him up, then fishes for
the friar's sword and hands it to him.

                                        CAMERA MOVES UP TO:

124.   TWO SHOT   ROBIN AND FRIAR TUCK

FRIAR TUCK (astonished):
> By our lady, you're the fairest swordsman I've ever
> met!

He again puts himself in fighting pose.

ROBIN (does not raise his blade):
> Must we go on? I think we're even.

FRIAR TUCK:
> Even? Nay—you're still ahead of me by half a leg of
> mutton! So—

He becomes belligerent again.

ROBIN (laughing, shakes his head):
> No—enough! Come with me, and I'll promise you
> the finest venison pasty—and the biggest—you ever
> ate! Boar, beef, casks of ale . . .

FRIAR TUCK (grumbling):
> If you'd said that before you'd have saved us both
> a wetting. Come along, then!

ROBIN (delighted):
> You'll join us?

FRIAR TUCK:
> Aye—if only to convert you from your thieving
> ways.

They clasp hands and go together out of the stream,
CAMERA PANNING with them. They talk as they go.

FRIAR TUCK:
You're Robin Hood, aren't you?

ROBIN:
How did you know?

FRIAR TUCK (chuckles):
If I hadn't known, you'd have gotten *this*—(taps his knife) through your ribs on your first trip across!

Robin looks at him as if to say, "Why, you double-dealing old so-and-so!" but Friar Tuck meets his glare with a bland smile which draws an answering appreciative grin from Robin. They climb the bank together. The outlaws crowd around and greet Friar Tuck with hearty claps on the back—all but Little John. •

125.   MED. CLOSE SHOT   THE GROUP
Little John surveys Friar Tuck's vast midriff.

LITTLE JOHN:
He's well-named Friar Tuck, Robin! (Points to the friar's big paunch.) It'll take half the deer in Sherwood to fill that cavern!

FRIAR TUCK:
And twice that to fill your empty head!

They glare at each other while the outlaws roar with laughter.

126.   MED. SHOT   ROBIN, FRIAR TUCK, AND OUTLAWS
still laughing, as they begin to leave the riverbank. Then, suddenly, they halt as they hear rapid hoofbeats. As they look off, CAMERA PANS to Will Scarlet, mounted as he approaches and rides into their midst.

WILL (urgent):
Robin! I've got word of—

He sees Friar Tuck and stops abruptly—

ROBIN:
It's all right. He's one of us.

WILL (surveys the friar):
One of us? He looks like three of us.

FRIAR TUCK (belligerently):
Aye—and equal to a dozen!

ROBIN (soothing):
Now—now— (Introduces them.) Friar Tuck—Will
Scarlet . . . (They acknowledge.) What is it, Will?

WILL:
Sir Guy of Gisbourne has started his return to Nottingham. He's stopping by the way tonight . . .

ROBIN:
Has he the tax money with him?

WILL (nods):
A fortune!

ROBIN:
When does he enter Sherwood?

WILL:
Tomorrow.

ROBIN (wide smile, to Friar Tuck):
Marvelous! We'll have to postpone that stuffing
match I promised you, good friar . . . (confiden-
tially), but I'll promise you a double one by this
time tomorrow. (To men.) Now, back to camp!

The outlaws cheer and move off.

127.   REVERSE SHOT   ROBIN AND HIS MEN
as they leave the river. Little John and Friar Tuck look
each other up and down with suspicious and disparag-
ing glances, like jealous mastiffs.

DISSOLVE TO:

128.   THE CAPTURE OF SIR GUY, LADY MARIAN, THE SHERIFF
       OF NOTTINGHAM, AND RETINUE

129.   ROBIN HOOD AND HIS MEN
       are shown advancing, carrying ropes covered with vines.
       As Robin Hood's men prepare, throwing them over the
       branches of the large trees, we CUT TO the following
       MONTAGE:

130.   A. BRANCH OF TREE   CLOSE SHOT
       as a coil of rope slithers up over it, falling on the other
       side.

131.   B. TREE   MED. CLOSE SHOT
       as the other end of rope drops into scene. Men catch it,
       pull it taut. A man starts winding vines around the rope.

132.   C. ANOTHER TREE   MED. CLOSE SHOT
       as several men swarm up it, one taking another vine-
       covered rope.

133.   D. SECTION OF BRUSH   MED. CLOSE SHOT
       Men are quickly moving into concealment in the
       shrubbery.

134.   E. FRIAR TUCK AND MUCH   MED. CLOSE SHOT
       Friar Tuck is squatting in the shrubbery, watching alertly.
       Much comes quickly into scene, crouching.

MUCH:
    See anything of 'em?

FRIAR TUCK:
    Not yet. Is everything ready?

MUCH (grins and nods):
    They'll think they got into a bloomin' 'ornet's nest.

As he starts to settle down beside Friar Tuck, he suddenly looks off scene, eagerly alert.

MUCH:
> There they come.

Friar Tuck looks CAMERA LEFT.

135.   FULL SHOT   SIR GUY'S RETINUE   SHERWOOD FOREST   DAY
as the retinue enters Sherwood Forest on the march to Nottingham. The retinue is in two parts. The first consists of an advance guard of about forty men-at-arms, archers, mounted and on foot. They are about two hundred yards in advance of the second section, at the head of which are Sir Guy, Lady Marian, Bess, and the sheriff.[11] Immediately behind them, ten larger men-at-arms, guarding four rude, horse-drawn wagons, containing chests and bales. Immediately behind those wagons, the commissary wagons, cooks, servants.
> CUT TO:

136.   LONG SHOT
Scene with the big trees in foreground, showing the advance troops coming into view and starting across the big field.
> CUT TO:

137.   CLOSER SHOTS
of advance guard.

138.   MED. CLOSE SHOT   AT TUCK AND MUCH
as they swiftly duck off scene in the direction of the woods toward which the troops are advancing.
> CUT TO:

138A.   LONG SHOT   SECOND SECTION
led by Sir Guy and Marian in woods.

139.   MED. CLOSE SHOT   LITTLE JOHN
concealed in the shrubbery, watching alertly.

140.   MED. CLOSE TRUCK SHOT   MARIAN, SIR GUY, AND HIGH
        SHERIFF
        as the high sheriff rides up. They are coming to a Z turn
        in the road, and already the tail of the leading party is
        disappearing around the bend.

        HIGH SHERIFF:
            Had-hadn't we better put out f-flanking guards?

        SIR GUY:
            What for?

        HIGH SHERIFF:
            Well . . . This is Sherwood, you know, and—and
            Robin . . .

        SIR GUY (curtly):
            Afraid of that gallows face?

        HIGH SHERIFF (indignantly):
            Afraid? Certainly not. (Looks nervously around.)
            But it's here that he's boldest—

        SIR GUY (scornfully):
            Don't worry. We're more than enough to take care
            of him. (To Marian, contemptuous laugh.) Outlaws
            have no stomach to show themselves against armed
            troops.

        MARIAN:
            Are you sure? I seem to remember—

        SIR GUY:
            Oh, he jumps out of ambush at small parties. But—
                                                        CUT TO:

141.   TRUCK SHOT SEQUENCE
        of dialogue between sheriff, Sir Guy, and Lady Marian.
        After line " . . . he wouldn't dare to attack us,"
                                                        CUT TO:

142.　MED. CLOSE SHOT　LITTLE JOHN
He gives a grim smile, then sees something to the rear
of Sir Guy's group.

CUT TO:

143.　SHOT
in woods of treasure wagon rumbling along.

CUT TO:

144.　MED. CLOSE SHOT　LITTLE JOHN
He ducks swiftly off scene.

CUT TO:

145.　LONG SIDE SHOT
across water of Sir Guy's group riding into water.

CUT TO:

145A.　FRONT SHOT
as they stop and let their horses drink.

146.　MED. CLOSE SHOT　WILL SCARLET
He is concealed in shrubbery watching them, CAMERA
LEFT, evidently pleased that they have stopped. He turns
in the opposite direction to look CAMERA RIGHT.

CUT TO:

147.　LONG SHOT　FROM REAR
of the advance troops disappearing into trees far across
field, leaving scene empty. Perhaps will have to use SHOT
of end of entire procession for this.

CUT TO:

148.　MED. CLOSE SHOT　WILL SCARLET
as he swiftly and silently exits from scene through brush.

149.　MED. SHOT　WOODS　ROBIN HOOD
Robin is in scene with several men who are quickly gathering up their arms, getting ready for the attack. Much
and Friar Tuck have already reported. Little John has just
arrived and is speaking:

LITTLE JOHN:
They're in two sections.

ROBIN:
> Where's Sir Guy?

LITTLE JOHN:
> Leading the second one. He has the treasure wagon
> with *him*.

ROBIN (an ironic smile):
> He would have.

WILL SCARLET'S VOICE:
> Robin! (He runs in.) Sir Guy and the sheriff have
> stopped at the river—watering their horses. The ad-
> vance guard's way ahead!

Robin turns to his men, who are all hidden up in the
treetops.

ROBIN:
> Are you ready, men!

CUT TO:

149A.   MEN
hidden in trees.

MEN'S VOICES:
> Let them come!

By this time the advance guard has arrived under the
trees, and we go now to a

150.   MONTAGE (OF APPROXIMATELY TWELVE CUTS)
ROBIN HOOD'S MEN
jumping and swinging off trees, thus overwhelmingly
capturing the advance guard. This to be INTERCUT with
shots of the second section led by Sir Guy, Lady Marian,
and the sheriff progressing on their route not aware of
what is happening to the advance section. All of a sudden the sheriff looks up and sees:

SHERIFF:
> Look!

CUT TO:

151. MED. LONG SHOT STRUGGLE BETWEEN ROBIN HOOD'S
      MEN AND THE FIRST SECTION

                                        CUT BACK TO:

152. SIR GUY AND THE SECOND SECTION
      Sir Guy is just about to give an order to his men when
      he finds himself in the same dilemma as the first section,
      as from all directions Robin Hood's men, jumping and
      swinging from the trees, overpower them. (THIS SHOT in
      some kind of a MONTAGE of about ten or fifteen cuts.)

153. MED. CLOSE SHOT MARIAN, SIR GUY, BESS, AND HIGH
      SHERIFF
      as their horses rear and lunge in confusion. They gradu-
      ally get them under control, and Bess moves close to
      Marian as though to protect her. They all see someone
      off scene and stare.

154. THEIR ANGLE SIDE OF THE ROAD
      Robin is standing easily at the edge of the shrubbery
      gazing at Marian. His friends are behind him. He un-
      covers and bows.

      ROBIN (sardonic amusement):
          Welcome to Sherwood, my lady. (His eyes flick Sir
          Guy.) Well, Sir Guy—haven't you a greeting for
          me?

      Sir Guy glares but does not speak.

      ROBIN (to Marian, mock puzzlement):
          That's curious . . . I hear he's often said he'd give
          me a warm welcome if we met again.

      MARIAN (furious, to Sir Guy):
          Are you going to go without even . . .

      ROBIN:
          Fighting? I'm afraid he has no choice.

Bess moves her horse forward, between Robin and Marian.

BESS:
> Well, *I* 'ave, you impident rascal . . . and you're not going to 'urt *my* lamb, my 'oneysuckle!

MARIAN:
> Be still, Bess!

Robin, grinning, motions Much to remove Bess. Much grasps her horse's head and leads her off. Little John, Will Scarlet, and Allan-a-Dale seize the bridles of Sir Guy, his squire, and the high sheriff, while the other outlaws hustle the men-at-arms into the woods and take charge of the caravan, servants, etc. Robin places himself at the head of Marian's horse and they all start moving into the forest.

DISSOLVE TO:

155.   MED. CLOSE MOVING SHOT   DAY
ROBIN, MARIAN, SIR GUY, AND PARTY
as they wind deviously through the woods. Sir Guy is looking from side to side, as though noting the way they are coming. Will sees this and nudges Robin to look. They exchange understanding grins.

ROBIN (to Sir Guy):
> Don't bother to mark the way. It'll take keener men than you've got to find our camp again!

SIR GUY:
> You'll hang for this! All of you!

ROBIN:
> You hear that, Will? Well, why aren't you shivering, you callous rascal!

Will gives a prodigious, ostentatious yawn, pats his mouth. To Sir Guy with exaggerated courtesy:

WILL:
Pardon *me*!

ROBIN (smiles and turns to Marian):
Hanging would be a small price to pay for the company of such a charming lady. You *are* charming, aren't you?

MARIAN (cool contempt):
What can a Saxon hedge-robber know of charm . . . or ladies?

WILL:
She means you.

ROBIN (mock surprise):
Me—a hedge-robber? *Tck-tck!* (Leans closer.) Tell me more about myself. You may have been misinformed.

MARIAN (icy):
Perhaps . . . but I don't find it interesting enough to bother about.

Robin grins, but she turns her head away, ignoring him. Will chortles.

156.   MED. CLOSE TRUCK SHOT   BESS AND MUCH
as he leads her horse through the woods. Bess is indignant.

BESS (tartly):
You just 'arm an 'air of me lady's 'ead and that ugly fice o' yours'll be walkin' about wi' no neck under it! Now mind!

Much does not answer. He just turns around, while walking, and stares at her.

BESS:
Well—wot are you starin' at?

MUCH (slow, embarrassed; grins, self-consciously):
I never been out walking with a—a female before.

BESS (startled, looks hastily about):
What female?

MUCH (gulps):
You.

BESS:
Well, of all the impidence! (Pause.) I s'pose you tells
that to all the girls!

MUCH:
I ain't ever had one.

BESS (interested):
You 'aven't? Why, you pore— (Recollects, says severely.) Well, you don't deserve none! (Sniffs.) A
houtlaw wot goes about robbin' people and knockin'
'em on the 'ead! (Pause.) You mean—you never
'ad one single sweet'eart in your life? (Much nods.
She, firmly.) You dunno wot you've missed, my lad.
(Proudly.) I've 'ad the banns up five times!

MUCH (incredulous admiration):
You have?

BESS (indignant):
Yes *I* 'ave! First time was a groom to my lord of
Cumberland . . . a very 'andsome rascal 'e was, too,
but unreliable. The second one . . .

As she talks,

SLOW DISSOLVE TO:

157.   MED. SHOT   ROBIN'S CAMP   AFTERNOON
Robin's outlaws are pulling rich costumes from Sir Guy's
baggage wagons and throwing them to their fellows and
to a half dozen ragged recruits, who throw off their tat-
ters and don the finery, parading and strutting, with
much laughter. Will Scarlet superintends the scene.
Nearby are some of Sir Guy's men-at-arms.

117

WILL SCARLET (to men-at-arms, indicates recruits' rags):
Come on—put 'em on! Robin's orders!

They reluctantly obey. Will picks up a handful of rags
and looks off scene.

WILL (calls, grinning):
Much!

As he throws the rags,

CAMERA SWIFTLY PANS TO:

158. MED. CLOSE SHOT   OUTLAWS AND CAPTIVES
as Much catches the bundle of rags thrown by Will, and
turns to a group composed of the high sheriff, Sir Guy,
Dickon, Friar Tuck, and Little John, as well as other outlaws and a few of Sir Guy's men, the latter partly un-
clothed and donning nondescript clothing. The high
sheriff's armor is half off, Sir Guy stands in cold, murderous rage as Little John forces him to take off his apparel. Friar Tuck, broadsword in hand, is superintending
the armor shedding of the high sheriff. Much dances
around everywhere, distributing rags. Dickon too is
partially disrobed of his uniform.

FRIAR TUCK (to high sheriff):
Hurry up! Get it off!

The high sheriff hurls a piece of armor down and stops,
close to tears of rage and mortification.

HIGH SHERIFF:
I won't! I—

Friar Tuck whangs him across the backside with his
sword.

FRIAR TUCK (politely):
Beg pardon?

The high sheriff hastily resumes his disrobing. Little
John has nearly finished disrobing Sir Guy, who, through

it all, retains his air of cold and dangerous menace. Much throws Dickon some rags.

LITTLE JOHN (solicitously):
You're quite sure you *really* want to wear these . . .

He hands up the filthy rags he is pressing on Sir Guy. The latter's eyes flame, but he does not answer. Much, who is donning the high sheriff's discarded apparel, looks up with a grin.

MUCH (to Little John):
Don't talk so silly! *Of course* 'e wants to wear 'em. It'll make 'im think 'e's a man! Besides, 'e'll enjoy prancin' barefoot through the dew.

LITTLE JOHN (bows to Much):
Well, my lord high sheriff, as a close friend of his, you should know!

Friar Tuck is squeezing into Dickon's gear (or other suitably ridiculous and ill-fitting garments), Much is completing his attire as the high sheriff, and Little John inserts his mighty, bulging frame into the clothes of Sir Guy. They strut and enjoy themselves. CAMERA PULLS BACK and reveals other groups exchanging clothes and rags with the men-at-arms. The outlaws are gay and laughing, having a grand time.

159. MED. SHOT SECTION OF GLADE WITH TABLE AFTERNOON
Long, rough tables have been set in a row down the length of the glade. In foreground two whole steers and several pigs are being turned on spits over fiery pits by outlaws under the bustling supervision of Bordo. Outlaws in finery are moving through background, thoroughly enjoying themselves, already beginning to gather near the tables, some hungrily taking a morsel of food.

160. MED. CLOSE SHOT MARIAN AND ROBIN
as they look at the scene. Marian is cold, an unwilling

prisoner, refusing to talk. Robin watches the peasants, smiling, forgetful of Marian for the moment.

ROBIN (softly):
> To them—(indicates serfs) this is a night in heaven.[12]
> Silks for rags . . . kindness, instead of whips . . .
> unlimited food, instead of hunger. Why—(exhilarated) they're actually *happy!*

MARIAN (indifferent and icy):
> Are they?

ROBIN (looks at her sidewise, curiously):
> Aren't you even a little pleased to see them enjoying themselves?

MARIAN:
> 'I think it's revolting!

ROBIN (slowly, gently, almost pitying):
> Your life has been very sheltered, hasn't it, my lady
> . . . ? Too sheltered, perhaps. If you could know
> them as I know them. Their infinite patience and
> goodness . . . their loyalty . . .

Marian glances at him, touched in spite of herself and puzzled at what strange manner of man he is. As she looks at him, Robin again intent and smiling at the scene before him,

161. MED. CLOSE SHOT   ROASTING PITS
Bordo punches his finger into the side of a crisping pig and licks it with a satisfied beam. He turns and bellows.

BORDO:
> To the tables, everybody . . . and stuff yourselves!

162. MED. SHOT   GLADE
as outlaws, people, and captives come flocking from every direction toward the table.

163.   MED. CLOSE SHOT   ROBIN AND MARIAN
as the people pass them on the way to the table.

ROBIN:
Now we'll sit down.

He gestures to the head of the table, but she does not respond. Instead, she is staring, indignant, off scene. As he turns,

CAMERA PANS TO:

164.   MED. SHOT   THE GLADE
Coming toward CAMERA, guarded by Friar Tuck and Little John, are three of the most bedraggled, ludicrous figures imaginable. Dressed in ragged sacking, barefoot, with wreaths of fern on their heads, and, a last ludicrous touch, a jaunty quill feather perking up out of each wreath, Sir Guy, the sheriff, and Sir Guy's squire are escorted by Little John, Friar Tuck, and Much, in their respective victim's gear.

165.   MED. CLOSE SHOT   MARIAN AND ROBIN
SHOOTING TOWARD the approaching figures. She stares, not knowing whether to cry or rage or laugh. But the ludicrousness of it is too much for her, and she begins to laugh, tries to control herself, is unsuccessful, and goes off into paroxysms of helpless, almost hysterical mirth. Sir Guy, Dickon, and high sheriff approach, followed by the grinning Friar Tuck, Much, and Little John. Robin, too, wears a broad smile. Sir Guy is apoplectic with fury and humiliation.

SIR GUY (to Marian):
Do I look so funny then, my lady . . .

Marian looks at him, wipes her streaming eyes, then goes off into more gales of laughter. Sir Guy and the high sheriff glare at her and each other; gradually Marian gets control of herself, although whenever she looks at them she has to fight to keep down little bubbles of mirth.

MARIAN (gasps):
I'm s-sorry—b-but you do look f-f-funny . . .

SIR GUY (to Robin):
I'll pay you out for this if it takes the rest of my life.

HIGH SHERIFF:
M-m-m-me, too!

ROBIN:
You should be grateful, my friends. Everyone knows that laughter's a sauce for good food.

He leads Marian out of scene, followed reluctantly by Sir Guy, the high sheriff, and Dickon, under the prodding of their captors.

DISSOLVE TO:

166.   MED. SHOT   HEAD OF TABLE
Robin and Marian are seated, with Will Scarlet on Robin's other hand. The other principals are scattered in places nearby, with Much and Bess the farthest away from the head of this immediate grouping. Sir Guy's men-at-arms and liveried servants are serving food, encouraged none too gently by outlaws. Of the captives only Dickon is eating.

ROBIN (to Marian):
May I serve you . . . ?

He gestures to a servant to place more food before her.

MARIAN:
I'm afraid the company has spoiled my appetite.

Will Scarlet stifles a laugh at this and gets Robin's heel under the table. He reacts indignantly and Robin smiles.

167. MED. CLOSE SHOT   HEAD OF TABLE   FROM A DIFFERENT ANGLE

embracing Friar Tuck, Little John, Much, Bess, Sir Guy, the high sheriff, and Dickon.

LITTLE JOHN (to Much):
> I seem to detect an odor of overripe meat, my lord sheriff . . .

Much sniffs, then looks at their captives, significantly, and back to Little John.

MUCH (lordly forbearance):
> It's only a whiff of the barnyard, Sir Knight.

He nudges Bess at this witticism, and she snickers admiringly. Friar Tuck, who has been wading into the food, looks up at this, glances around, then notices that the high sheriff isn't eating. He pokes him, points to the food. The high sheriff glares at him in disgust. Little John empties the sheriff's plate into his own and again wades in.

CAMERA PANS TO:

168. TABLE   MED. SHOT

as the whole crowd falls to with a will. Sir Guy's servants, herded by outlaws, bustle back and forth in acute nervousness and fear, lugging an unending stream of platters of steaming food from the cooking pits. Four or five outlaws, lolling against trees, play stringed music and sing as a background to the feast.

CAMERA TRUCKS UP TO:

169. ROBIN AND MARIAN   MED. CLOSE SHOT

as Robin offers to serve some meat to Marian.

ROBIN:
> Will you have some of this?

MARIAN (emphasizing each word):
> I said—I'm not hungry!

Robin gives a faint smile and says no more, helping himself lavishly with a will and falling to eating with keen enjoyment, paying no attention to her. After an instant Marian's eyes glance across at his plate of food, and it is plain that she is tempted. She withdraws her eyes with an effort and looks down the table. As she does, her lips compress.

170. TWO SHOT   MUCH AND BESS
sitting together at the table. Much is leaning back, his mouth open, while Bess holds suspended over it a juicy piece of meat. As she drops it in his mouth, he pretends to bite her. She coyly slaps him, harder than she had intended. He straightens, gulps, nearly chokes, and lifts up his hand to slap her back. She grabs a knife and threatens him. They look at each other, then both smile. There's a bit of infatuation going on here. He steals his arm around her waist. She promptly jabs his hand with her knife point, and he snatches it away and sucks it. He grins fatuously and again playfully smacks her. As she heartily smacks back her eyes go beyond, and she straightens primly.

171. MED. SHOT   MARIAN   FROM BESS'S ANGLE
glaring along the table at her. Bess slaps away Much's hand, which is attempting to squeeze her.

BESS (affected modesty and indignation):
    Be'ave yourself, you 'orrible creature!

She turns back to her meal, subdued, with nervous side glances at Marian and a sly smile for Much.

172. CLOSE PAN   TRUCK SHOT   FRIAR TUCK'S PLATE
We see Friar Tuck's hand listlessly drop a half-eaten meat bone back on the table, and we PAN UP AND BACK as the friar leans slowly back, his hands going to his stomach.

FRIAR TUCK (groaning):
Oh . . . *me!*

The SHOT REVEALS Sir Guy, sheriff, Dickon, and Little John beyond them. Sir Guy and the sheriff are sitting in silent rage; they have touched nothing. Little John is still munching slowly and contentedly. He looks across the two silent men at the friar.

LITTLE JOHN:
I'm ashamed of you.

FRIAR TUCK:
I'm ashamed of myself. No appetite anymore. (Shakes his head and sighs.) I must be getting old. (Addresses high sheriff, points to his untouched plate, which a servant has replenished.) Do you live off the fat in your head, my friend? (The friar offers him a great meat rib.) Come—just tickle your gizzard with this!

The high sheriff turns away in disgust, but as Friar Tuck lowers the bone he gazes at it with longing, and his tongue flicks his lips. Little John and Friar Tuck exchange grins.[13]

DISSOLVE TO:

173. ROBIN   CLOSE PAN SHOT
He is still eating, slowly, and looking off scene at Marian in silent amusement. The CAMERA PANS OVER, revealing Marian, unaware that he is looking at her, silently and earnestly eating. She sees him looking at her and stops.

174. MED. CLOSE SHOT   AT TWO
Robin smiles and rises. Marian watches him.

175. MED. FULL SHOT   TABLE
Robin speaks, in an easy, bantering tone.

ROBIN:

> My friends, I had supposed with you that Sir Guy
> . . . (looks at Guy and bows) was a scurvy fellow.
> Yet he provides this tasty supper. (As he speaks, a
> train of men carrying heavy boxes approaches and
> sets them on the table before Robin and his friends.)
> But is this the end of his beneficence? Ah, no! For
> in his train today he's brought us half a score of
> boxes . . . jewels, silks, and about thirty thousand
> golden marks wrested from the northern shires!

SIR GUY (jumps to his feet):

> You wouldn't dare—

He is pulled down by Little John.

ROBIN:

> You might think that our noble host intended this
> treasure for the coffers of Prince John instead of to
> ransom the king . . . (pause) and you'd be right!
> But a change of heart overtook him in the forest
> . . . (points to boxes) and there it is, safe and sound.

There are cheers from the outlaws. Marian looks up.

MARIAN (contemptuous):

> You, talk of loyalty!

176.   MED. CLOSE SHOT   MARIAN AND ROBIN
as he looks down.

ROBIN:

> Yes. Why not?

MARIAN (sarcastic):

> I suppose you and your band of cutthroats intend
> to send this treasure to Richard. You wouldn't *dream*
> of keeping it yourselves . . .

ROBIN (smiles):

> Oh—I see . . .

He turns again to his men and signals for silence.

ROBIN:

> Tell me . . . what do we do with this treasure? Divide it among ourselves? Or—

The outlaws, in a voice of thunder, give decision.

OUTLAWS (ad lib):

> Keep it for Richard! It belongs to the king! Send it for his ransom! (Fanatic loyalty.) A Lion-Heart . . . ! A Lion-Heart!

Robin turns, looks at Marian with a smile that says more than words, and sits down again.

177. TWO SHOT   ROBIN AND MARIAN   FROM A DIFFERENT ANGLE

ROBIN:

> Convinced?

MARIAN:

> I may have been—hasty. But why you—a knight, should live here like an animal in the forest . . . robbing . . . killing . . . outlawed . . .

ROBIN:

> And you wonder why? (She nods.) It would take long to explain. But . . .

As he speaks he looks off, watches something.

178. MED. LONG SHOT   TWO OUTLAWS   FROM ROBIN'S ANGLE
They are carrying platters of food from the table toward the forest.

179. MED. CLOSE SHOT   ROBIN AND MARIAN
as he turns back to her.

ROBIN (slowly):

> Would you really like to know why I turned outlaw? Or are you afraid of the truth . . . or of me . . . ?

MARIAN:
I'm afraid of nothing! Least of all, of you!

ROBIN (rising):
Come with me, then!

As she hesitates, then rises and follows him,

180. MED. CLOSE SHOT   SIR GUY AND HIGH SHERIFF
The high sheriff nudges Sir Guy and indicates Robin and
Marian as they pass in background. Sir Guy turns to
look, then starts to get to his feet. Friar Tuck and Little
John slam him down again, and grin at each other.

DISSOLVE TO:

181. MED. CLOSE SHOT   ROBIN AND MARIAN
in a little cleared space over which interlaced branches
form a close-knit canopy. The two outlaws have reached
the place and are giving food to five or six prone figures—sick, gaunt, tortured faces, flayed backs, blind,
etc. Seeing Robin they stretch out their hands from their
pallets, in grateful greetings, clasping his hand. But seeing Marian with him, they say nothing.

ROBIN (cheerfully):
Well, my friends, you'll soon be on your feet again,
eh?

There are grateful murmurs of assent.

CAMERA MOVES UP TO:

182. TWO SHOT   ROBIN AND MARIAN
As she looks down at the sick men with pity and horror,
Robin speaks quietly.

ROBIN:
Blinded . . . tongues slit . . . ears hacked off—tortured . . . (He meets her horrified gaze.) Once
these—creatures—were   villagers—serfs—happy
and contented. (Pause.) Now they seek refuge with
me . . . (gestures back toward camp) from your
Norman friends . . .

Marian looks at the men for a few seconds without speaking. When she looks back at Robin, her eyes are moist. He takes her by the arm and leads her away.

183. MED. CLOSE SHOT   ROBIN AND MARIAN
on the bank of a stream.

MARIAN (low):
But you've taken Norman lives.

ROBIN:
Only the cruel and unjust. (Quietly.) That (jerks his head back, indicating the place of the sick men) wasn't pleasant . . . but perhaps you'll remember—and understand.

They sit down. It is a peaceful and lovely place, with the late sun slanting through the trees.

MARIAN (low):
You're a strange man . . .

ROBIN:
Strange . . . because I can feel for helpless, beaten people?

MARIAN (swiftly):
No . . . ! Strange, because you want to do something about it. Because you're willing to defy Sir Guy—even Prince John himself—to risk your own life . . . (pause) and one of those men there was a Norman . . . I can't understand—you, a Saxon . . .

ROBIN (shakes his head impatiently):
Saxon . . . Norman . . . what does that matter? We're all Englishmen! It's injustice I hate, not the Normans!

MARIAN:
But it's lost you your rank, your lands . . . made you a hunted outlaw when you might have lived in comfort—security. What's your reward for . . . (raises her hands, palms upward) all this?

ROBIN (incredulous):
> *My reward . . . ?* (Looks curiously at her again.) You
> just don't understand, do you?

MARIAN:
> I'm sorry . . . ! (Impulsively puts her hand on his.)
> Yes . . . I do begin to see . . . a little . . . now . . .

She stands and he follows, faces her.

ROBIN (slowly):
> If that's true . . . then I want no greater reward . . .

They look at each other, quiet, deadly serious, the shell
of race hostility stripped for a moment from them both.
For one vital second they are drawn each other by the
almost irresistible alchemy of attraction, and it seems almost as though they would embrace. But each holds rig-
idly in and the tense moment passes. She holds out her
hand, and he puts it to his lips. Then, together they turn
back toward the camp.

DISSOLVE TO:

184.　MED. SHOT　　　　　　　　　LATE AFTERNOON
THE TREASURE AND COMMISSARY WAGONS
Sir Guy and the high sheriff, under guard, are standing
at the wagons, Sir Guy watching with jealous rage as
Robin and Marian enter the scene. The glade behind
them is a background of music, revelry, laughter. Much
and Bess in background. CAMERA PANS with Robin and
Marian as they join the group.

SIR GUY:
> Now that you've robbed us and had your fill of in-
> sulting us, we wish to leave. (To Marian.) Come,
> Marian . . .

ROBIN:
> My own men will escort my lady. But before you
> bid her good night you might thank her for saving
> your life.

SIR GUY:
> My life?

ROBIN (smoothly):
> Do you think you'd have left this forest alive if the
> Lady Marian hadn't been with you?

Robin turns to two of his men, Harold Broadbutt and
Saint Peter.

ROBIN:
> Harold! . . . Peter! (They come forward.) Take six
> men and guide our gallant host and his nervous
> friend to the Nottingham Road.

SIR GUY:
> But our horses . . . ! Our clothes!

ROBIN (clipped and curt):
> You'll return to Nottingham as you are . . . on foot,
> to teach you humility . . . and perhaps a little mercy!
> (To Sir Guy.) The rest of your people will be re-
> turned tomorrow.

SIR GUY (helpless, raging; looks at Marian):
> But the lady . . .

Robin looks at Marian and smiles, then back to Sir Guy:

ROBIN:
> You'd better get started before I change my mind.

At this the sheriff plucks Sir Guy nervously by the arm
and starts off; Sir Guy gives the group one long deadly
stare, then slowly turns and follows. Robin watches them
with a grim smile, then turns to Marian.

ROBIN:
> And now, my lady—

He beckons Bess, who comes forward with Much. Then
he turns and looks off.

ROBIN (calls):
> Friar Tuck . . . ! Little John . . . !

They arrive at the group, pushing and shoving.

LITTLE JOHN AND FRIAR TUCK (together):
>Yes, Robin?

They glare at each other. Robin smiles.

ROBIN:
>You'll take the Lady Marian to the Abbey of the Black Canons for the night. It's halfway to Nottingham. Then tomorrow the bishop can give her escort the rest of the way. And watch out that the bishop's men don't take you!

Bess turns and looks coyly at Much. He comes eagerly forward.

MUCH:
>May I go too, master?

Robin nods, smiling at Marian, who returns his smile. Little John and Friar Tuck stare at Bess and Much, then exchange a look of utter disgust at such sentimentality. Robin starts off scene with Marian, the others following.

185. MED. CLOSE SHOT WAITING HORSES
As Robin leads Lady Marian in and helps her mount, Will, Friar Tuck, and Little John, gathering up their weapons, mount two other horses, Little John having to help the friar to mount. Bess, being helped on her horse by Much, slips, and he catches her in his arms, then finally boosts her on, so heartily that she almost goes off the other side. She simpers and primps at his gallantry.

186. CLOSE SHOT AT ROBIN AND MARIAN
as he helps her mount and stands looking up at her an instant.

ROBIN (quietly):
>Good-by . . . my lady . . .

MARIAN (looks at him):
>Good-by . . .

Robin stands watching, as they ride away. A little distance off Marian turns. Robin raises his hand and she responds. As he watches them,

FADE OUT

FADE IN

187.   INT. ROOM IN NOTTINGHAM CASTLE   DAY
Sir Guy and the high sheriff, dressed now in everyday costume, are facing Prince John, who is in a towering rage, pacing up and down.

PRINCE JOHN:
> He took everything you'd collected?

SIR GUY:
> Every silver penny!

PRINCE JOHN (angry roar):
> And you two nincompoops sat there and let him do it.

HIGH SHERIFF:
> But—but—we resisted as well as we could—

PRINCE JOHN (turns on him):
> Where are your wounds . . . ? your bruises? And where are your men?

HIGH SHERIFF:
> They're being returned today . . .

PRINCE JOHN:
> With not an arrow wound to divide among the lot of 'em, I suppose! And more than thirty thousand marks in the hands of that wolf's-head! (Beats fist into palm in impotent fury.) That fellow's *got* to be taken! (Glares at them both.) Understand?

SIR GUY:
> I agree with you—but how?

133

HIGH SHERIFF (eagerly):
We could muster an army and surround Sherwood . . .

SIR GUY (stops again):
You? You couldn't capture him if he sat in your lap
shooting arrows at a crow.

HIGH SHERIFF:
Arrow . . . arrow? That stirs something in my mind.
(Suddenly brightens as an idea hits him; he gets up
excitedly.) Listen—perhaps we can't take him by
force. He's too well protected . . . knows Sherwood's hidden paths too well. But . . .

He cogitates. Prince John is impatient.

PRINCE JOHN (snaps):
Well, out with it!

188.   CLOSE SHOT   HIGH SHERIFF
excited and triumphant.

HIGH SHERIFF:
We'll outtrick him! (Sir Guy gives him a contemptuous look.) Hold an archery tournament!

SIR GUY'S VOICE (sardonically):
And have him fly in on the end of one of his own
arrows! Marvelous!

HIGH SHERIFF:
Wait a minute . . . ! He's the finest archer in the
north. Do you think he'd forego the pleasure of
shooting against the archers of all England? Give a
prize, say, of a golden arrow . . .

189.   CLOSE SHOT   PRINCE JOHN

PRINCE JOHN:
. . . and ask him to risk his neck for that!

HIGH SHERIFF'S VOICE:
That won't be the only bait to draw him!

190.   THREE SHOT   SIR GUY, HIGH SHERIFF, AND PRINCE JOHN
as they look at the high sheriff with dawning interest.

HIGH SHERIFF:
Didn't you notice that when he and the Lady Marian
came back from the forest, she seemed friendly . . .
and how his eyes never left her?

SIR GUY (reluctantly):
I noticed.

HIGH SHERIFF:
Well, then . . .

SIR GUY:
But how'd we get word to him?

HIGH SHERIFF:
Get word to Robin—when he has eyes in every
bush, and . . . (looks around and lowers his voice)
ears in every wall?

PRINCE JOHN:
But even if he comes, won't he be disguised?

HIGH SHERIFF:
Whether he dresses as beggar or priest, knight or
palmer, what disguise can conceal the finest archer
in England? (Emphatically.) The man who wins the
golden arrow will be Robin Hood!

As they look at each other and smile,[14]

FADE OUT

FADE IN

191.   FULL SHOT   THE TOURNAMENT FIELD   DAY
Around three sides are erected tiers of seats for the spectators, with royal boxes and booths for the nobility and

gentry in the center. At one end of the field are pitched gaily colored tents, one for the archers of each knight. Above the tent of each knight is his colored banner bearing his heraldic device upon it. The stands are crowded with people and more are streaming in. Everywhere are the gaiety and brilliance of colored banners and ribbons fluttering against the blue sky. Near one end of the field, five targets are set up. The sides of the field are crowded with excited spectators.

192.   LONG SHOT   PAGE   GOLDEN ARROW ON CUSHION IN PROCESSION

193.   MED. SHOT   ROYAL BOX
Establishing bishop, Bess, Marian, Prince John, Sir Guy, and the sheriff.

194.   LONG SHOT   THROUGH BOX
Procession passing royal box.

195.   MED. SHOT   PRINCE JOHN, SIR GUY, AND SHERIFF
The sheriff beams ingratiatingly at Prince John.

SHERIFF:
I hope our little golden hook catches the fish.

PRINCE JOHN (a cold eye):
You hope.

SHERIFF (confused):
Oh . . . it will . . . if he's here.

PRINCE JOHN:
If he's not we'll stick your head upon the target and shoot at that.

The sheriff gulps.

SIR GUY:
Are your men sure of their orders?

196.   CLOSE SHOT   SHERIFF

SHERIFF:
> Yes . . . yes . . . they're stationed all around the
> field. A worm couldn't get through them.

197.   MED. CLOSE SHOT   MARIAN AND PRINCE JOHN
Both are looking off toward sheriff, Marian puzzled and
disturbed. Prince John gives a slight grunt as if to say,
"He'd better not."

MARIAN:
> You speak as if this were a trap.

PRINCE JOHN (turning blandly):
> No, my dear . . . just a precaution in case the Sax-
> ons make a disturbance.

He turns forward and gives a signal. Marian remains
uncertain and disturbed.

198.   UP ANGLE   TRUMPETERS
An effective up-shot of a line of trumpeters as they
SOUND a blast.

198A.   LONG SHOT   FIRST SHOT
Herald announcer riding from royal box to center of
field.

199.   UP ANGLE   HERALD
as he pulls to a stop and announces:

HERALD:
> By orders of His Highness Prince John, the cham-
> pion archers of Sir Guy and the knights will be lim-
> ited to three flights of arrows for the eliminations.
> The winning team will meet all comers.

He wheels horse, rearing out of scene.

200.   EXTREME LONG SHOT
of crowd cheering as herald rides back to box.

201.   HIGH LONG SHOT
Archers in line, waiting for signal.

202.   CLOSE-UP   PRINCE JOHN
gives signal.

203.   MED. SHOT
Official with sword signals archers.

204.   MED. SHOT
Archers shoot.

205.   MED. LONG SHOT
Arrows hit target.

206.   ROYAL BOX
as they watch, or SHOT OF CROWD, a timing cut.

207.   MED. CLOSE SHOT   REFEREE
as he walks in to last target and quickly counts it, then
turns.

REFEREE:
Prepare flight two.

He exits.

208.   MED. LONG SHOT
Archers shoot second time.

209.   CLOSE SHOT   MARIAN
as she follows flight of arrows. They thud and land off
scene. She catches sight of something else, first as if uncertain of recognition, then with realization and alarm,
her eyes following him.

209A. TRUCK SHOT   ROBIN AND HIS MEN
eliminating if possible the first line, "You're not going to enter this," etc.

LITTLE JOHN:
You know it's a trap.

ROBIN:
A golden arrow from the lady herself.

FRIAR TUCK:
They've cooked up this whole thing just to take you.

ROBIN:
Oh, well . . . what of it?

LITTLE JOHN:
You know what will happen if they do.

ROBIN:
Where is your sporting blood? Sir Guy accepted our invitation. We'd be rude not to accept his.

WILL:
It would be ruder to get your neck stretched.

ROBIN:
There you are! My band getting fat and overfed. Where's your love of fights, risk, adventure?

FRIAR TUCK:
Since our friend seems to have gone a little mad, I'll have to see him through.

LITTLE JOHN:
We'll have to see him through.

210. MED. SHOT   MARIAN, PRINCE JOHN, SIR GUY
She knows it is Robin, and from this instant on, remembering the conversation in the box, is terribly afraid for him, but tries to conceal it from the others. She gives a quick glance at the others to see if they have discovered

Robin. To her relief they are looking in another direction. She looks back toward Robin.

211. CLOSE-UP ROBIN
As he looks toward royal box in distance, his eyes crinkle in a faint, warm smile.

REFEREE'S VOICE:
Teams of Sir Guy of Gisbourne and Sir Mortimer leading eight and seven points. Prepare final flight.

Robin turns his gaze toward archers.

212. ARCHERS
shooting third flight.

213. CLOSE-UP ROBIN
as they watch the flight of the arrows.

214. MARIAN, PRINCE JOHN, SIR GUY
NOTE: We retake this scene, as Marian hadn't seen Robin and wasn't worried in the one already taken.[15]

Marian is watching Robin. She doesn't hear Sir Guy at first.

SIR GUY:
Does my lady find it interesting? (She doesn't hear him.) Lady Marian! (She turns, flustered, hiding her emotion.)

MARIAN:
Oh . . . I'm sorry.

SIR GUY:
I asked if you found it interesting?

MARIAN:
Yes . . . yes . . . very. They're . . . splendid archers.

SIR GUY:
You'll find it much more exciting later on.

Marian realizes the import but hides her feelings.

215.   CLOSE SHOT   REFEREE

REFEREE:
    Teams, one, two, four, and five eliminated. High
    score—nine points, to Sir Guy of Gisbourne's team.
    It will remain in competition.

    Applause from off scene.

216.   SHOT   ATTENDANTS
    running in and taking arrows from targets, starting just
    after arrows have landed.

217.   UP ANGLE   TRUMPETERS
    as they sound a blast.

218.   CLOSE SHOT   HERALD
    as he calls.

    HERALD:
    The winning team will shoot as individuals . . .

219.   CLOSE PAN SHOT   SIR GUY'S TEAM
    CAMERA REVEALS Phillip of Arras standing looking at the
    course with good, egotistical contempt.

    HERALD'S VOICE:
        Captain—Phillip of Arras—

    CAMERA REVEALS Elwyn.

    HERALD'S VOICE:
        Elwyn the Welshman—

    CAMERA PANS to third man.

    HERALD'S VOICE:
        Matt of Sleaford. They now challenge all comers!

220.   CLOSE SHOT   WILL AND SOME OF ROBIN'S MEN
dropping first two lines and starting with

PEDDLER:
Eh. The man who shoots against that lot'll have to
have the eyes of a falcon!

COUNTRYMAN:
Aye. They're too good for me. I'm not shooting
today.

221.   CLOSE SHOT   HERALD

HERALD:
Step up, ye bold bowmen of England, and see who
will carry off the prize!

222.   MED. SHOT   CROWD
Archers pass onto field.

223.   CLOSE SHOT   FRIAR TUCK AND LITTLE JOHN
and others start onto field.

224.   CLOSE SHOT   ROBIN
knocks off guard's helmet.

225.   MED. SHOT   ROBIN
and some of his men pass from line in front of guards.
DOLLY ONTO FIELD.

226.   MED. LONG SHOT   ROBIN
and his men, Little John, and others, preparing to shoot.

227.   PRINCE JOHN, SIR GUY, AND SHERIFF
Sir Guy and sheriff are leaning forward, studying the
group off scene with alert interest. Prince John, leaning
back, is also looking. He turns to Sir Guy.

PRINCE JOHN:
Have you found our elusive friend?

SIR GUY (grimly):
Not yet . . . but we will.

228.   CLOSE SHOT   PHILLIP
He prepares to shoot with the others as a single trumpet
blast comes into scene.

229.   LONG SHOT
from back of targets. Archers shoot.

230.   MED. SHOT   ARCHERS
change position. Robin steps to foreground, looks toward royal box, then shoots.

231.   CLOSE SHOT   MARIAN
watching fixedly, trying to hide her fear.

232.   MED. SHOT   ATTENDANTS
taking arrows out of targets.

232A.   CLOSE SHOT   LITTLE JOHN AND FRIAR TRUCK
using only first two lines.

LITTLE JOHN:
Move your fat carcass, my friend, and make room
for a man.

FRIAR TUCK:
There'll be room enough between our arrows for
ten such fatheads as you.

233.   CLOSE SHOT   PHILLIP OF ARRAS
as he shoots.

234.   TARGET
NOTE: From the time Robin and others enter competition, we should use trick camera angles on arrows as
suggested by [Howard] Hill, emphasizing speed and
impact. If possible, get a few arrows coming directly to-

ward camera lens, hitting just above it in rubber pad attached on front of camera.

The target has about twenty arrows in it. Phillip's smacks into center of others.

DISSOLVE TO:

235.   TARGET
with four arrows in it, two in center, two an inch away. A hand is pulling out the two outer ones. The referee's voice times with him.

REFEREE'S VOICE:
Matt of Sleaford, out . . . Elwyn, the Welshman, out!

236.   MED. CLOSE SHOT   GROUP OF FOUR
as Matt and Elwyn leave, Elwyn throwing away his bow in surly disgust. Robin and Phillip are left standing alone.

237.   PRINCE JOHN, SIR GUY, SHERIFF, AND LADY MARIAN
The three men are leaning forward eagerly. Marian is motionless, fearful, as we come to scene. Prince John leans back with satisfaction.

PRINCE JOHN:
Ah—the tinker.

SIR GUY:
I'll take him now.

He starts to signal, but Prince John interrupts.

PRINCE JOHN:
Not so hasty. I'm enjoying it. Let them finish the match.

SIR GUY (angry, expostulating):
But he—

PRINCE JOHN:
Have your men close in if you wish.

238. CLOSE-UP   SIR GUY
giving a signal.

239. CLOSE-UP   DICKON
signals to guard.

240. CLOSE SHOT   FRIAR TUCK AND LITTLE JOHN
Guards press past them.

241. CLOSE-UP   WILL
looking worried.

242. SHOT OF GUARDS
moving through crowd.

243. CLOSE SHOT   ROBIN
As he selects an arrow, he glances around out of the corner of his eye.

244. MED. CLOSE SHOT   SECTION OF CROWD
as two or three soldiers casually ease through to the front of the crowd.

245. CLOSE SHOT   ROBIN
as he gives a faint smile and shoots.

246. MED. CLOSE SHOT   TARGET
as Robin's arrow smacks into the dead center of the empty target. A cheer from the crowd.

247. CLOSE SHOT   MARIAN AND PRINCE JOHN

PRINCE JOHN:
Very good. (To Marian.) Would you say you'd seen that tall fellow before?

MARIAN (disdainful):
If I had . . . what interest could a tinker have for me?

Prince John smiles and turns his attention to the field.

248.   PHILLIP SHOOTS

249.   MED. CLOSE SHOT   TARGET
His arrow smacks into center right beside Robin's. It is a tie.

250.   CLOSE SHOT   REFEREE

REFEREE:
A tie. You will be allowed another flight.

251.   ROBIN, PHILLIP, AND MARSHAL
deciding to move the target further.

252.   PRINCE JOHN AND SIR GUY

PRINCE JOHN:
If your archer captain wins at that distance, I'll give you a thousand gold marks for him.

SIR GUY:
Win or lose, I will *give* him to Your Highness . . .

253.   CLOSE-UP   MARIAN
Sir Guy's voice continuing into scene.

SIR GUY'S VOICE (continuing):
. . . for a favor . . . provided you let me deal with the wolf's-head in my own way.

254.   TWO SHOT   PRINCE JOHN AND SIR GUY

PRINCE JOHN:
I am leaving for Norwich immediately after the tournament anyway, so you may do what you please with him.

255. MED. SHOT   PHILLIP
shoots his final shot.

256. TARGET
Arrow hits dead center. Cheer from crowd.

257. TWO SHOT   SHERIFF AND SIR GUY

SHERIFF:
Why, he *can't* win now. No living man can beat that
shot. I'll wager a hundred marks on Phillip of Arras.

258. MED. SHOT   ROBIN
picks a long arrow and shoots.

259. TARGET
Robin's arrow splits Phillip's arrow and remains in target as two halves of first arrow fall. Hysterical cheering
off scene.

260. THREE SHOT   ROYAL BOX   MARIAN, PRINCE JOHN, AND
SIR GUY

261. MED. LONG SHOT   CROWD
cheers.

262. LONG SHOT   DOLLY   CROWD
picks up Robin and starts for royal box.

263. CLOSE-UP   MARIAN

264. CLOSE SHOT   FRIAR TUCK AND LITTLE JOHN
Guards press past them.

265. CLOSE-UP   WILL
looking worried.

266.   TIE-UP LONG SHOT   CROWD
drops Robin to ground in front of royal box.

267.   CLOSE SHOT   ROBIN
bows to royal box.

268.   THREE SHOT   MARIAN, PRINCE JOHN, AND SIR GUY

PRINCE JOHN:
What is your name, archer?

269.   CLOSE-UP   ROBIN

ROBIN:
Godfrey o' Sherwood, Your Highness.

270.   CLOSE-UP   PRINCE JOHN

PRINCE JOHN:
How is it that a tinker learned so well the use of arms?

271.   CLOSE-UP   ROBIN

ROBIN:
Even a peaceful tinker must protect himself these days, Your Highness, from treachery and other unpleasant things.

272.   CLOSE-UP   PRINCE JOHN

PRINCE JOHN:
It's earned you more than you bargained for today.

273.   THREE SHOT   MARIAN, PRINCE JOHN, AND SIR GUY
Prince John rises and says:

PRINCE JOHN:
I pronounce you champion archer of England, and from the gracious hand of Lady Marian Fitzwalter, you will receive your reward.

Page brings the arrow to Lady Marian.

PRINCE JOHN (continuing):
Advance!

274. MED. CLOSE-UP ROBIN
steps forward.

275. TIE-UP MED. SHOT ROBIN, PRINCE JOHN, LADY MARIAN,
AND SIR GUY

MARIAN:
I—

276. CLOSE-UP MARIAN

MARIAN:
I—here's your prize, Sir Archer.

277. CLOSE-UP ROBIN

ROBIN:
It is indeed an honor to receive it from the hands of
so beautiful a lady.

278. CLOSE SHOT SIR GUY
He speaks with slow venom, wasting no time on byplay.

SIR GUY:
How is it you didn't use a black arrow today?

279. CLOSE SHOT ROBIN

ROBIN:
That's my court of last resort, Sir Guy. Its verdict is
always final.

280. GROUP SHOT

SIR GUY:
Arrest this man!

This scene should be reshot because Robin should not hesitate and half turn as if planning to go the other way but discovering the way barred. As Sir Guy speaks, Robin should, as if he had planned this strange way out beforehand, leap on Sir Guy, knocking him down with a crash, hurling a couple out of the way in the back line and dart to the back curtains, jerking them apart, leaving pandemonium in his wake.[16]

281.   MED. CLOSE   REAR OF BOX   AT CURTAINS
as he jerks them apart, preparing to leap out, but stopping as he sees his way cut off.

282.   REVERSE ANGLE   HIS ANGLE
Eight or ten guards are rushing toward rear of box.

283.   INT. BOX   MED. CLOSE SHOT
as Robin quickly darts away from curtains and darts off scene.

284.   MED. SHOT   ROBIN   AT FAR END   BACK OF PAVILION
As he runs along, another ring of horsemen appear suddenly from around the end of the pavilion and close in on him.

285.   FULL SHOT   BACK OF PAVILION
Mounted soldiers in unbroken ranks are closing in on Robin from three sides. He slides to a stop, looks desperately for a way of escape, then, with a bound, he ducks back into the rear of the pavilion.

286.   PAN SHOT   ROBIN
as he dashes to the front of the pavilion again. When he is seen, a roar goes up from the crowd. Two solid files of mounted men-at-arms ride in from the flanks cutting off his escape. From every side, men-at-arms appear and make for him. He stands, cornered, as they close in on him.

287.   MED. CLOSE SHOT   PRINCE JOHN, SIR GUY, AND PARTY
in the royal box, watching the troops close in on Robin.
Marian is horrified. Sir Guy has a sardonic smile. The
high sheriff is jubilant. Prince John is complacent.

288.   MED. CLOSE SHOT   ROBIN
fighting as the men-at-arms rush him. He is ringed now
in a solid trap of steel. He fights desperately but they
bear him down. The mob is yelling and fighting on the
field. The men-at-arms pinion Robin's arms and drag
him toward the royal box.

289.   MED. CLOSE SHOT   ROYAL BOX
as Robin is dragged before Sir Guy and Prince John.
Robin is bleeding and tattered. Sir Guy looks at him,
from head to foot, with a contemptuous smile, then
reaches out and strikes him heavily across the face.

SHERIFF:
That's a very good idea!

As he too reaches forward to strike, Robin launches out
with his foot and gives him a terrific kick in the belly.

HIGH SHERIFF (gasps in agony):
Oof!

He staggers backward and falls on his rear, then sits
there, gasping and holding his guts.

ROBIN (to Prince John):
Your turn now, Your Highness!

PRINCE JOHN:
You're a very rash young man, and I'm sorry I can't
remain in Nottingham to see what Gisbourne has
in store for you. It'll be something special, I'm sure!

ROBIN:
No doubt. (To Sir Guy.) Sorry I underestimated you.
Next time—

SIR GUY:
There'll be no next time for you. (To men-at-arms.)
Lock him up!

As Robin is led away,

290. CLOSE SHOT   MARIAN
She stares after him, dread in her eyes, then she turns.
CAMERA PULLS BACK TO:

291. TWO SHOT   MARIAN AND SIR GUY   PRINCE JOHN IN
BACKGROUND

He is watching her sardonically. As she turns away from
him, and he and Prince John exchange mordantly
amused glances,
FADE OUT

FADE IN

292. MED. SHOT   GREAT HALL OF NOTTINGHAM CASTLE   NIGHT
Robin, heavily guarded by men-at-arms under Dickon,
is standing before Sir Guy. He and Sir Geoffrey, Sir Mortimer, Sir Ralf, and the high sheriff are sitting as a tri-
bunal. Marian is present, with other Norman ladies.
Marian's face is set—emotionless. Sir Guy has a paper
before him. Robin is dirty, tattered, blood stained.

SIR GUY (reading):
"Robin of Locksley, known to some as the outlaw
Robin Hood . . . after a fair trial in which you were
not able to produce one witness on your behalf, you
have been found guilty of outlawry, theft, murder,
abduction, false pretenses, contempt of the Crown,
poaching in the royal forests, and high treason."

ROBIN (coolly):
Haven't you forgotten a count or two?

SIR GUY:
What do you mean?

ROBIN:
> Isn't it a crime under the noble Prince John to love
> my country . . . ? A felony to protect the serfs against
> your rapacity . . . ? A misdemeanor to be loyal to
> my king?

SIR GUY:
> If I could add anything to the charges against you,
> I'd gladly do so! (Picks up paper again.) "It is the
> sentence of this tribunal, that on the morrow, at
> high noon, you be taken to the town square of Not-
> tingham, and there hanged by the neck till you are
> dead." (Leans forward.) There may be some . . .
> (his glance rests briefly on Marian, who gives no
> sign) who will regret that a man of your peculiar
> talents should be cut off so early in life. But person-
> ally . . .

ROBIN (contemptuously):
> . . . you think the sentence exceedingly lenient.
> (Sardonically.) I thank you!

Robin turns to the men-at-arms.[17]

293.   MED. CLOSE SHOT   ROBIN, SIR GUY, AND MARIAN
as Robin is led past. Robin does not look at her. Marian
stares straight ahead. Sir Guy's eyes rest on her, narrowly watching for some sign of emotion. He is disap-
pointed. As he gets up and the others rise,

DISSOLVE TO:

294.   MED. CLOSE SHOT   ROBIN   NIGHT
as his guards, headed by Dickon, halt at a dungeon
door. A turnkey opens it, and Robin is thrust inside.

295.   MED. CLOSE SHOT   DUNGEON   NIGHT
It is unfurnished, there being not even a cot, only chains
bolted into the wall. Robin is shoved inside and followed by Dickon and men-at-arms, and his hands and
feet are chained to the wall. As the men-at-arms turn

and exit, closing the door and leaving Robin in total
darkness,

WIPE TO:

296.   MED. SHOT   INT. MARIAN'S APARTMENT   NIGHT
Marian and Bess. Marian is at the window, back to CAM-
ERA, her closed fist beating in tiny impotent, desperate
blows against the frame. She turns, eyes filled with tears,
and paces a step or two, registering intense apprehension. Bess is watching her.

BESS (tenderly):
> What's—what's troublin' you, me lady? Is—is it the
> outlaw?

MARIAN:
> Yes. I—I hate to see . . . to see any human being
> trapped and—and— (Desperate resolve.) Bess . . .
> you know where his men may be found, don't you?

BESS (startled and uncertain):
> Why, me lady, 'ow would I know—

MARIAN (impatient, desperate):
> Don't put me off! . . . That—that little man who—
> who liked you. You've been seeing him? (Bess nods.)
> Tell me where!

BESS:
> You want to get a message—

MARIAN:
> —to his band! Yes!

BESS:
> Well, me lady, I *'ave* 'ad a nip of ale of a night, now
> and again, at a place in the town, and I won't deny
> as some of the others was there—

MARIAN (agony of suspense):
> Where was it?

BESS:

> It's a tavern . . . the Saracen's Head in Pilgrim Court.
> The landlord's name is Humility Prin. Knock on the
> door and say: "A Locksley." But—

MARIAN:

> Get me a cloak—quickly!

As Bess runs for the cloak,

DISSOLVE TO:

297. MED. SHOT STREET IN NOTTINGHAM NIGHT

Marian is hurrying along in the shadows. Three
drunken men-at-arms approach, singing tipsily. As she
passes, one of them grabs at her. She tears loose and
runs. They stare owlishly after her and one starts in pursuit, but his companions pull him back.[18]

DISSOLVE TO:

298. FULL SHOT ROOM IN THE SARACEN'S HEAD NIGHT

A low, dimly lit beamed room. It is crowded with Robin's
outlaws, among them Little John, Will Scarlet, Allan-a-
Dale, Much, and Friar Tuck. They are worried and rest-
less. Many sit with their heads in their hands. One man
goes to the window and draws back the heavy drape to
look out. Another shoves him roughly out of the way
and replaces it.

WILL SCARLET (beats his fist in his hand):

> There must be *some* way—

LITTLE JOHN:

> Why can't we batter the place down?

FRIAR TUCK:

> You'd need a siege engine to even dent it.

ALLAN-A-DALE:

> He'll be hanged for sure. But perhaps on his way to
> the gallows we might—

WILL SCARLET:
> With three hundred men to guard him? Maybe Little John's right. We should—

There is a low rap at the door and every man straightens, tense, his hand flying to his weapon. The door opens and Humility Prin, the tavern keeper, enters. He is a powerful, squat man with a lugubrious squint and a heavily pockmarked face.

WILL SCARLET:
> What is it, Prin?

PRIN:
> A lady—the Lady Marian!

WILL SCARLET (incredulous):
> Wha-at?

LITTLE JOHN (angry growl):
> It's a trap! Watch them windows!

Several of the outlaws, with drawn weapons and bows ready, run to the windows.

PRIN (lugubrious shake of the head):
> She'd the password right enough.

WILL SCARLET:
> Is she alone? (Prin nods.) Fetch her in!

Prin goes to the door and beckons and Marian enters. There is an instant angry murmur from the outlaws.

WILL SCARLET:
> What do you want here, my lady?

299. MED. SHOT THE GROUP
as Marian approaches them. She is nervous but determined.

MARIAN:
> I want to help him!

WILL SCARLET:
How did you find us here?

MARIAN:
Never mind that now! Oh, please—don't stand there staring! Tell me what I can do!

OUTLAW (from window):
Don't trust her! It's another Norman trick!

SECOND OUTLAW:
He's right! She'll have the lot of them down on us!

MARIAN (desperately):
Would I come here alone if it was a trap? What's to prevent you keeping me here, or killing me, if— (Despair.) Is there *no* one here with sense enough to see—

FRIAR TUCK (waddles forward):
Just a minute! (The others fall back; to Marian, gently.) We've got to make sure, my child. (Pause.) You're a good daughter of the church? (Marian nods; Friar Tuck raises his crucifix.) You swear by this holy cross you want to help Robin?

MARIAN (touches the crucifix earnestly):
I swear, good father!

Friar Tuck looks at her long and earnestly. There are tears in her eyes. He turns to the others.

FRIAR TUCK:
Have you thought of anything?

MARIAN:
Yes! (They cluster around her.)

LITTLE JOHN (growl):
Can you get us into the castle?

MARIAN:
> That would do no good. He's too heavily guarded.
> I've thought of another way. Listen to me . . .

She talks rapidly.

DISSOLVE TO:

300. FULL SHOT   MARKET SQUARE NOTTINGHAM   DAY
Bells are tolling in the town. A great mass of people is congregated around the gallows platform, held back a few yards by ranks of men-at-arms. In close alignment on three sides of the gallows platform are mounted men-at-arms, their horses facing outward toward the crowd. More men-at-arms on foot push callously through the sullen, angry crowd. The hangman mounts the gallows steps and the crowd roars derision and insults. The men-at-arms strike, to silence them. A few yards from the gallows, a pavilion has been erected for Sir Guy and his knights, and they, with Marian and Norman ladies, are already in place.

CAMERA MOVES UP TO:

301. MED. SHOT   SIR GUY'S PAVILION
He is sitting with Marian, other women, the high sheriff, and several Norman knights. Marian is keyed up, but tries to look unconcerned. There is excited, ad lib conversation.

HIGH SHERIFF (rubs his hands):
> This is a rare treat, eh, my lady?

MARIAN (looks at him, coldly):
> Yes—isn't it?

Sir Guy looks at her.

SIR GUY:
> With him out of the way we'll quickly stamp out the rest. (Smiles.) And to think I was foolish enough to believe that you liked—(puts his hand on hers) why, your hands are cold as ice . . .

He is interrupted by the sudden, resentful roar of the crowd. They turn their heads to look.

CAMERA PANS TO:

302. MED. LONG SHOT   ROBIN AND HIS GUARDS
He is standing, half naked, hands bound behind him, in a small mule-drawn cart which advances under heavy guard and flanked on each side by mounted men-at-arms, out of a street onto the square. The cart turns and begins a circuit of the square.

303. CLOSE SHOT   MARIAN
as she looks at Robin. Her hands tug furtively at her kerchief, and her head turns with the progress of the cart.

304. MOVING SHOT   ROBIN
as he is drawn in the cart. His head is up, his face calm. There are ad lib murmurs of sympathy from the crowd, which is held firmly back by men-at-arms who line the route.

CROWD (ad lib):
Bless you, Robin! We'll not forget you, lad! We'll fix 'em for this some day! Etc., etc. . . .

The cart comes abreast of Sir Guy's box, and Robin gazes straight at Marian. Sir Guy looks swiftly from Robin to her, but she gives no sign. The cart stops.

ROBIN (gaily, to driver):
What are you stopping for? What's ahead—(jerks his chin at gallows) is a pleasanter sight than this!

The cart moves on.

305. MED. SHOT   THE SQUARE
SHOOTING toward the gallows as Robin's cart turns toward the side of the scaffold platform, which has been left vacant by the horsemen already in position.

306.   CLOSE SHOT   MARIAN
She watches Robin in an agony of suspense.

307.   MED. SHOT   GALLOWS PLATFORM
as Robin's cart reaches it and is backed around. A man-at-arms drops the tail gate and Robin steps onto the platform.

308.   MED. CLOSE SHOT   ROBIN
SHOOTING past the hangman's cruel, bony face, as Robin steps onto the platform and calmly looks around him. He sees Sir Guy and gives an ironical, mocking salute.

309.   TWO SHOT   SIR GUY AND HIGH SHERIFF

SIR GUY (coolly):
   He'll not be so insolent when they've stretched his neck!

They look back at Robin, then their faces react in astonishment and horror.

310.   MED. SHOT   THE GALLOWS PLATFORM
Robin walks swiftly forward, across the platform, past the hangman, under the noose, and then, with a sudden spring, onto the saddle of one of the men-at-arms in the rank facing outward on the far side of the platform. Immediately Robin's rider and those flanking him put their horses to the gallop and dart away, another of the men-at-arms riding close and slashing his bonds.

311.   MED. CLOSE SHOT   SIR GUY, HIGH SHERIFF, AND KNIGHTS
as they jump in consternation to their feet. The jubilant roar of the crowd rises in waves.

HIGH SHERIFF:
   Wha-wha-wha—?

SIR GUY (yells):
   Stop him! Stop him!

160

312.   MED. SHOT   GALLOWS PLATFORM
Two mounted men-at-arms (Robin's men) obstruct the
efforts of their companions to pursue. The crowd breaks
through the guards and immediately there is welter,
confusion, and fighting.

313.   CLOSE SHOT   MARIAN
She is watching, with mingled fear and jubilation,
pounding her fist softly into the other palm as she sees
Robin and his friends ride toward safety. Instinctively
she grips Sir Guy's hand, but he, mistaking her emotion, covers her hand with his, while he watches, furious
and intent.

314.   PAN SHOT   ROBIN AND FRIENDS
as they gallop hell-for-leather through the streets toward
the gate. Suddenly out of a side street come two mounted
men-at-arms leading another horse with empty saddle.
They swing alongside Robin and party, and Robin at full
gallop leaps into the empty saddle. The party rushes on.

315.   MED. SHOT   INT. TOWN GATE OF NOTTINGHAM
It is a portcullis, lowered and guarded by men-at-arms.
Nearby are numerous carts, horses, etc., left by country
people who have gone to the square for the hanging. A
half dozen men, serfs, countrymen, etc. are lounging
about, one watering the horses, another arranging sacks
on a cart, etc. A serf passes, carrying a bale of fodder.

MAN-AT-ARMS (grins):
Why aren't you at the execution, Saxon? Afraid the
hangman'll recognize you?

Suddenly hoofbeats come over the scene. The men-at-
arms stiffen. The serf with the fodder drops it, looks
swiftly around at the other serfs, raises his hand as a
signal, then leaps like a cat on the back of the man-at-
arms, bludgeoning him down. At the same instant the

other men hanging about jump on the guards with sword and knife. There is a brief fight; then, with the men-at-arms beaten, the serfs, etc. run to the portcullis and quickly wind it up. Robin and his friends gallop through. The serfs and others jump on horses tethered nearby and follow. As they do, they jubilantly shed their peasant jerkins, etc. and reveal themselves in Lincoln green. As they gallop along the road after Robin and the others,

FADE OUT

FADE IN

316.   MED. SHOT   NIGHT
       INT. MARIAN'S APARTMENT IN CASTLE

as the door opens and Marian enters followed by Bess, who is carrying Marian's tapestry frame.

BESS:
> Where would you like it, me lady?

MARIAN (indicates spot):
> Here—near this good light.

As Bess carries the frame, she hums contentedly to herself.

MARIAN (smiles):
> Why, Bess . . . I haven't heard you sing since . . . (speculatively) let me see . . . (recollects) not since the time we were captured in Sherwood—

BESS:
> It ain't me habit to sing, me lady, 'less I've got something to sing about!

MARIAN:
> But . . . being captured's a queer reason . . . (goes to tapestry frame and begins to work on it) and what's the special reason today?

BESS (shrewdly):
> P'raps the same reason my lady's happier lookin' than I've seen her for weeks.

MARIAN:
You mean—you think I'm glad because the—the wolf's-head escaped?

BESS (looks steadily at her):
You didn't shed no tears, mum, when he got away— 'less they was tears o' happiness.

MARIAN (turns to her, indignant):
What do you mean? How dare you! Just because I felt sorry . . .

317. CLOSE SHOT BESS

BESS (starts tidying the room, says calmly):
It's no good tryin' to deceive me, me lady, what took you from your poor mother's arms, and loved you, and spanked you out of yer infant tantrums till you was as pink as a beet from your 'ead to yer—

MARIAN'S VOICE:
Bess!

BESS (imperturbable):
It's nothing to be ashamed of. A delicate skin like yours gets red very easy. I wish the young man you're in love with was a bit 'andsomer, to match you.

MARIAN'S VOICE (indignantly):
He *is* handsome! (Bess smiles as if to say: "I told you so.") And I'm *not* in love with him!

BESS (sagely):
Love's what I'd call it, me lady—and though you might not think it to look at me now—(smirks a bit) I ain't been without me experiences.

318. CLOSE SHOT MARIAN

MARIAN (severely):
Well, you're mistaken . . . and don't be ridiculous!

(Pauses, softly.) Bess . . . (Bess looks at her.) You *do* think he's handsome, don't you?

BESS (judicially):
> As men go . . . yes, me lady! (Pause.) And you are a bit fond of 'im, aren't you?

MARIAN (slowly):
> I don't know . . . (Pause.) Stop that silly moving about and talk to me!

BESS (submissively):
> Yes, me lady.

As she crosses and stands near Marian.[19]

319.   TWO SHOT   MARIAN AND BESS
Marian turns to her, her hands folded in her lap.

MARIAN (hesitant):
> You know—he's different from anyone I've known . . . he's brave . . . reckless . . . yet gentle, too . . . kind . . . not brutal like— (She leaves the thought unsaid.) Tell me . . . When you *are* in love does it— I mean—is it hard to—to think of anything but one person . . . ?

BESS (authoritatively):
> Yes, indeed, me lady . . . and sometimes there's a bit of trouble sleeping . . .

MARIAN (softly):
> I know . . . but it's a nice kind of not sleeping . . .

BESS:
> And it affects yer appetite—though I 'aven't noticed it's done that to you, 'cept when he was in the dungeon, going to be hanged . . .

MARIAN (eagerly):
> And does it make you want to be with him all the time . . . ?

BESS (also eagerly):
> That's right, and when you are with 'im your legs is
> like water and—and—tell me, me lady—when 'e
> looks at you do you get prickly feelings, like goose
> pimples, sort of, running up and down yer spine?

Marian nods excitedly.

BESS (solemnly):
> Oh, then there's not a doubt of it!

MARIAN:
> Doubt of what?

ROBIN'S VOICE:
> . . . That you're in love!

As they both look off, startled, and Marian jumps to her
feet,

320.   MED. SHOT   THE ROOM   SHOOTING FROM BEHIND
MARIAN
as Robin leaves the shelter of some drapes and advances
into the room. Over his Lincoln green he wears a long,
ragged, palmer's cloak, and a palmer's round hat is on
his head, its brim hung with tiny, dangling effigies of
the saints and bearing a cross of palm leaf. His face has
been made grimy, and it is difficult to recognize him.
We realize that in darkness or semidarkness his disguise
would be complete.

MARIAN (sharp, terrified):
> What do you want—? (Sudden realization.) Oh . . .
> Robin!

Bess, who has been frightened stiff, begins to recover
and is indignant at Robin's frightening Marian.

BESS (indignantly bridles):
> Well, I must say—(anger rises) I *must* say . . .

MARIAN (swiftly):
>   Keep quiet, Bess. (Bess subsides; to Robin.) Are you
>   completely mad? (He nods, cheerfully.) Why did
>   you come here?

321.   MED. SHOT   MARIAN AND ROBIN
Bess moves to background.

ROBIN:
>   To see you.

MARIAN:
>   But don't you realize . . .

ROBIN:
>   When I got back to the forest my men told me how
>   much I owe you. So I came at once to thank you—
>   and after what I just overheard—(she glares at him)
>   I'm *very* glad I came!

MARIAN:
>   What you just heard was—was a game. You've got
>   to go! At once!

ROBIN:
>   A game? Well—now that I'm here couldn't *we* play
>   it a little? (Deprecatingly.) Of course I haven't the
>   charm—(looks at Bess, who bridles) of that young
>   woman . . . (Bess, mollified, puts on a flattered sim-
>   per) but I'd do my best.

MARIAN (worried still; to Bess):
>   Bess—leave us, please.

Bess exits, looking with fond approval at the two. Robin
flashes her a smile as she goes, then turns back to Marian.
As he speaks,

CAMERA MOVES UP TO:

322.   TWO SHOT   ROBIN AND MARIAN[20]

ROBIN:

How do we begin? (Recalls.) She said—(gestures
after Bess) "There's no doubt of it!" And *you* said—
(points index finger at Marian) "No doubt of what?"
. . . And *I* said (points thumb at himself): "That
you're in love." (Looks into her eyes.) Right so far?
Now you say: "Who am I in love with . . . ?" And I
say: "With me!" Why, it's very simple! (Seriously.)
You *are* in love with me, aren't you, Marian, because—(he checks her protest) I'm terribly in love
with you. That's really why I came. I had to see you
again.

MARIAN (hard):

You've got to go! At once! And—and I don't love
you!

ROBIN:

You *don't*? You're sure?

MARIAN:

Yes!

ROBIN (shrugs):

All right—then I'll go!

He crosses to the window, CAMERA PANNING with him,
and throws one leg over, then looks down.

CAMERA PULLS BACK TO:

323.   MED. CLOSE SHOT   ROBIN AND MARIAN

Marian instinctively starts forward to stop him, then
checks, frightened.

ROBIN (looks down into courtyard):

Now let me see . . . (Strokes his chin.) There's a fat
captain of the guard, with bowlegs. If I dropped on
him, it'd make 'em worse. Or there's a mounted
archer—but that'd be hard on the horse—

MARIAN (appeal and worry):
Robin . . .

ROBIN:
And—ah! the very thing . . . ! Five men-at-arms talking in a group. (Starts to climb out.) They'd break the fall beautifully . . .

MARIAN (cries out):
Robin . . . !

ROBIN (checks, looks at her, says politely):
Yes?

MARIAN:
Please.

Robin climbs in the room again and moves swiftly to her.

ROBIN:
Then you do—? (She is silent.) Don't you? (Shakes her.) *Don't* you?

She looks up at him and nods, close to tears. He takes her in his arms and holds her close. As he kisses her,

DISSOLVE TO:

324. MED. SHOT ROOM IN NOTTINGHAM CASTLE NIGHT
Sir Guy, the high sheriff, Sir Mortimer, and Sir Ralf in one group facing Sir Geoffrey. The latter is stained with the dust of travel.

SIR GUY (to Sir Mortimer):
Any luck?

SIR GEOFFREY:
We searched every hamlet, every rick, every cottage.

He shrugs helplessly and takes up a horn of ale.

SIR GUY (nasty):
But not Sherwood, of course!

SIR GEOFFREY (just as nasty):
Give me an army of five thousand and I'll do that.

HIGH SHERIFF:
I should have gone myself! I'd have got somebody
to show me the way to him.

SIR GEOFFREY (to high sheriff):
You did find him once . . . (malicious glance at Sir
Guy) or have you forgotten?

SIR GUY (brusquely):
Never mind that! We let Locksley escape, and we've
got to—

SIR MORTIMER (angrily):
We let him escape? You had charge of him.

SIR GUY:
Aye—but if I'd had some knights with their wits
about 'em . . .

SIR MORTIMER:
You've always boasted you were worth six men.
What did you need us for?

Sir Guy, in a fury, draws his sword, and Sir Mortimer
leaps to meet him. Sir Geoffrey thrusts between them,
the sheriff, petrified with fear, dancing on the outskirts.

HIGH SHERIFF (stammers):
N-n-now, gentlemen . . . n-n-no violence!

SIR GEOFFREY (thrusts between, curtly):
Better save your tempers for the outlaw—when you
catch him again!

HIGH SHERIFF (relieved):
That's a very good idea! (Scratches his head, gab-
bily.) But what passes my understanding is—

SIR GUY (sourly):
If we discussed everything that passes your understanding before we caught him we'd die of old age!

As he strides away,[21]

325. MED. CLOSE SHOT   ROBIN AND MARIAN   NIGHT
sitting on a divan in her castle apartment. They are terribly in love. Robin is lying back, looking at her.

ROBIN:
Tell me . . . (She looks at him.) Why did I fall in
love with you?

MARIAN (indignant):
Why—don't you know?

ROBIN:
It must have been your temper! (Reflectively.) I love
women with tempers!

MARIAN:
Do you know you're very impudent?

ROBIN (grins):
Am I?

MARIAN (firmly):
You *are*!

                        CAMERA MOVES UP TO:
326. TWO SHOT   ROBIN AND MARIAN
She glares at him in mock anger, then goes on:

MARIAN:
And when my *real* guardian, King Richard, finds
out—

ROBIN:
Finds out what?

MARIAN (impatiently):
About you being in love with me . . .

ROBIN:
I know! He'll make me court jester!

MARIAN:
He won't! He'll stick your funny head on London gate!

ROBIN:
To wink at the London girls, my bold Norman beauty!

MARIAN:
I'm not bold!

ROBIN:
But you *are* Norman— (Magnanimously.) Oh, I don't hold that against you—(her chin goes up; he wheedles) and you *are* a beauty!

Marian gets up. Robin follows her.

MARIAN (fiercely):
And you are leaving here—at once . . . (She silences his protest.) Please, darling! Every minute you're here you're in danger—(she clings to him) you've *got* to go now!

ROBIN (gazes at her):
I wonder . . . (Pause; then gently.) Marian—will you come with me?

MARIAN:
To Sherwood?

ROBIN:
Yes . . . (Earnestly.) I've nothing to offer you but a life of danger—and myself. We'd be hunted . . . endure hardships . . . but we'd be together.

MARIAN:
But Robin, dear—

ROBIN:

I know. It's asking a lot . . . but who knows how
long it may be, before— (Breaks off, then gently.)
Father Tuck could marry us; and when Richard
returns . . . (Looks deep into her eyes.) Will
you . . . ?

MARIAN:

Because I love you, Robin, I'd love it, too—even the
danger, if you were with me . . .

ROBIN:

Then you will?

MARIAN (shakes her head):

No. (Puts her hand gently on his arm as if pleading
for understanding.) Listen to me, darling . . . (draws
him again to divan and they sit down) that night in
Sherwood I realized for the first time that what you
were doing was right, and we were wrong. (He
would interrupt but she checks him.) No—let me
finish! You taught me then that England is bigger
than just Normans and Saxons fighting, hating each
other! It belongs to all of us, to live peacefully together . . . loyal only to Richard and England!

ROBIN:

But you could help—

MARIAN (her hand on his lips):

I could help more by watching for treachery here
and leaving you free to protect Richard's people, till
he returns. (Gently.) Now do you see why you have
to go back to your men—alone?

He looks at her, infinite love and admiration in his eyes,
then bends and kisses her. Then he turns to leave, but
returns after a step or two and sweeps her again into his
arms. They cling in desperate, heartbreaking embrace.

327.   MED. SHOT   HALL OUTSIDE MARIAN'S CHAMBERS

Sir Guy walks into the scene from around a corner and

approaches Marian's door, CAMERA PANNING with him. He is about to pass when he halts and stands, tense and listening. He nears the door, uncertain, and raises his hand as if to knock.

328. MED. CLOSE SHOT INT. MARIAN'S CHAMBERS
Marian and Robin are standing, frozen. Marian's fingers are on his lips, and his sword is half withdrawn. They listen and wait.

329. CLOSE SHOT SIR GUY
listening at Marian's door. He draws back, biting his lips. Listens again; then, with a shrug he turns and leaves, CAMERA PANNING with him. As he turns the corner,

330. TWO SHOT MARIAN AND ROBIN
They are still standing, listening, but her hand has dropped and he has returned his sword to his scabbard.

MARIAN:
Go now—quickly, sweetheart . . .

ROBIN (huskily):
Good-by, my darling . . .

MARIAN (low voice, face close to his):
Oh, Robin . . . is it wicked to be so terribly, *terribly* happy?

Robin kisses her again with infinite tenderness, then he goes to the window, Marian watching, and, CAMERA PANNING with him, puts his legs over the sill, grasps a stout vine, and draws himself swiftly up, out of sight. As Marian looks after him, her face radiant with love,

FADE OUT

FADE IN

331. INT. KENT ROAD TAVERN MED. SHOT
The inn is barren and has a look of poverty. The only cheer is a big fire that roars in the fireplace, casting

173

dancing shadows across the candle-lit room. The place
is deserted except for a lean, frail old man, the proprietor, who is just finishing serving meager food and drink
to five men who sit at a corner table dressed in long,
enveloping travelers' cloaks. They are King Richard, the
earl of Essex, and three other nobles, his chief men. We
do not learn their identity for awhile. The proprietor is
crossing to the table with the last of the plates as we
come to scene.

332. MED. CLOSE SHOT AT TABLE
as proprietor puts down plates.

PROPRIETOR:
You gentlemen have traveled far? (Essex nods.) I'm
sorry I can't give you better food. There is little left
to us these days.

RICHARD:
This will be enough.

FIRST KNIGHT:
The inn at Luton was well supplied. How is that?

PROPRIETOR (a faint, sad smile):
Ah . . . but that is a Norman inn. They are *all* pros-
perous. If it weren't for the help of our blessed Robin I would have had to close these doors long ago.

RICHARD (quick questioning):
Robin . . . ?

PROPRIETOR:
Robin Hood—the outlaw.

RICHARD (as if recollecting):
Oh, yes—yes! I understand he's quite a champion
of the Saxons.

PROPRIETOR:
He helps all people in distress . . . Saxon *or* Norman.

RICHARD (to Essex):
Queer sort of fellow, this Robin. (To proprietor.)
How does one find him?

The proprietor, like all others who love Robin and are
alert to defend him, immediately becomes suspicious
and shuts up like a clam.

PROPRIETOR (vaguely):
I've no idea . . . (Changing the subject.) Would you
gentlemen like some more of our good brown ale?

ESSEX:
If you please.

During the above few lines we hear hurried arrival and
commotion outside, growing loud on Essex's line. As
the proprietor starts to turn away from the table,

333.   MED. SHOT   TOWARD DOOR
as the Bishop of the Black Canons bursts in with five or
six of his monks. The bishop is in a towering fury; the
others look nervously at him and each other.

BISHOP:
I'll complain to Prince John. I'll have this rascal's
ears no matter how! He dares to rob *me*!

334.   MED. CLOSE SHOT   AT TABLE
The proprietor's face shows stark fear. The men notice
the expression and study the bishop off scene curiously
as he continues to rant.

BISHOP'S VOICE:
Strips *my person* of jewels! What's this country coming to when even a high churchman can't travel
through the forests in safety!

RICHARD (to proprietor, low-voiced):
Who is he?

PROPRIETOR:
The Bishop of the Black Canons.

335. MED. SHOT ROOM

MONK (to bishop):
Do you wish to go on after dinner, Your Grace?

The bishop gestures angrily to his men.

BISHOP:
No . . . ! We can't reach the abbey tonight! I'll stay
here. Tend to the horses! (They exit; he wheels on
proprietor.) Get food for us!

PROPRIETOR:
Yes, Your Grace . . . at once.

As he speaks, he hurries toward the kitchen. The bishop
turns toward the men at the table, wanting an audience
to complain to.

BISHOP:
It's no longer safe to journey anywhere. Robbers all
over.

RICHARD (courteously):
What happened, Your Grace?

336. CLOSE SHOT BISHOP
puffing and indignant. He sits down near them and draws
off his shoes, holding his feet to the blaze.

BISHOP:
I just told you! We were robbed! Not a chance to
defend ourselves! They burst on us from ambush—

RICHARD'S VOICE:
Who did?

BISHOP:
Why, Robin Hood, of course! There's no other rascal
with impudence enough—

ESSEX'S VOICE (low but audible):
Robin Hood. The same we were speaking of, sire!

At the word "sire," the Black Bishop looks sharply off, at Essex.

337.   INT. KENT ROAD TAVERN   MED. SHOT   NIGHT
as the Black Bishop, with growing suspicion, surveys Richard and his companions.

BLACK BISHOP:
You've heard of him, then?

RICHARD (indifferently):
He seems well known hereabouts.

BLACK BISHOP:
Ah! Then you're strange to this shire?

FIRST NOBLE:
More or less.

BLACK BISHOP:
And—what might your names be, gentlemen?

RICHARD:
They're hardly important enough to deserve the interest of Your Grace. (Looks around.) Landlord . . . where's our ale?

LANDLORD (entering from kitchen):
Coming, sirs . . .

The Black Bishop takes his rebuff in silence. The landlord brings the ale and sets it down before Richard and his companions, who finish their meal. The Black Bishop looks at them.

BLACK BISHOP:
Will—will you gentlemen be remaining here overnight?

ESSEX (coolly):
We hadn't decided, Your Grace. What would you advise?

BLACK BISHOP (dubious warning):
We-ell . . . with so much danger on the roads you'd be far safer staying here.

RICHARD:
We shall then . . . (the bishop starts drawing on his footgear again; Richard observes this, adds) since we'll have the added pleasure of your company.

BLACK BISHOP (looks up, embarrassed):
I—I—well, I'd really like to stay, but I've recollected some urgent affairs at my abbey. Another time . . . or perhaps . . . (stands up) you'll break your journey and sup with me tomorrow?

RICHARD (murmurs):
Your Grace is too kind . . .

The Black Bishop moves toward the door. Richard stands.

BLACK BISHOP:
Good night, gentlemen. I wish you Godspeed in the morning.

RICHARD:
Thank you. Good night. (To landlord.) Landlord!

The bishop goes out the door.

338.   CLOSE SHOT   BLACK BISHOP OUTSIDE ROOM DOOR
as he closes the door and listens against it intently.

RICHARD'S VOICE (from within):
Are there beds prepared, landlord? (Yawns loudly.) Let's turn in, then. I'm tired.

As the Black Bishop nods, satisfied, to himself, and hurriedly exits,

339.   MED. CLOSE SHOT   NIGHT
        RICHARD AND FRIENDS IN TAVERN
        They look at the door through which the Black Bishop
        left, then significantly at each other. Essex lifts a ques-
        tioning eyebrow at Richard, who nods, and sits down.

    RICHARD (grim smile):
        Yes, I'm afraid he suspects. So we'll give him a start,
        then we'll move on.

    ESSEX:
        His Grace is a Norman. Did you see the fear in the
        landlord's face when he came in?

    RICHARD (somberly):
        I've seen it in the faces of thousands since we re-
        turned. I should never have left England.

    SECOND NOBLE:
        I notice, though, that when Robin Hood's name is
        mentioned—

    FIRST NOBLE:
        Ah, yes—the mysterious outlaw . . . (To Richard.)
        Now, what about him?

    RICHARD (smiles):
        This bishop had no trouble in meeting him. It's
        given me an idea. (Rising.) Shall we go?

        As they rise, SOUND TRACK carries the noise of rapid
        hoofbeats. They freeze. Essex goes swiftly to a window
        and looks out, turns back to the room, jerks his head at
        the window, then, as the others crowd to look, again
        peers out the window.

    ESSEX:
        I think it's time for us to leave.

340.   MED. SHOT   CASTLE CORRIDOR   NIGHT
        outside the Great Hall, the doors of which are open. In
        background of scene is a circular stone stairway which

communicates with the upper floors of the castle, and also the dungeon. The scene is poorly lit and draughty.

NOTE: During this scene, at a dialogue point to be timed by the director so that the important parts of the dialogue will be overheard by her, Lady Marian will descend the stairway, pause, when she overhears the voices below, listen, when she realizes the import, then, toward the end of the scene, continue her descent around the pillar via the stairway, and out of scene.

CAMERA DISCOVERS Prince John, Sir Guy, and the Black Bishop talking. Dickon stands a few feet away, waiting. A man-at-arms, one of the castle guards, approaches the group, unhurriedly doing his sentry go.

PRINCE JOHN (to Black Bishop):
And you're sure— (He breaks off, looks at the approaching sentry, says testily.) Move yourself, man! Don't dawdle along! (The startled man-at-arms accelerates and moves rapidly past. To bishop.) You're *sure* it was Richard?

BLACK BISHOP:
No doubt of it, Your Highness. And one of those with him was Essex, and another, I *think*, was Pembroke.

CAMERA MOVES UP TO:

341.   MED. CLOSE SHOT   SIR GUY, PRINCE JOHN, AND BLACK BISHOP
Dickon is in background, and beyond him the stone stairway.

PRINCE JOHN (low, furious tone):
How like my dear brother this is! (Vitriolic.) He couldn't rot in Dürenstein,[22] like any decent man would . . . ! But no! He must pop up here, to spoil our game!

The Adventures of Robin Hood

SIR GUY:

>Spoil it? Why should he? (The others stare in astonishment. Smoothly.) Richard hasn't an army with him . . . If he had, we'd have heard of it.

As he continues to speak,

CAMERA MOVES UP TO:

342.   THREE SHOT   SIR GUY, PRINCE JOHN, AND BLACK BISHOP
Dickon and stairway in background. It may be at this point that Marian begins to descend. Dickon must be placed so that he does not observe her entrance. He watches intently the conference of his masters.

SIR GUY (low, cold, deliberate):

>Richard, you say, is stopping the night at this Kent Road Tavern? (Black Bishop nods.) Then if Richard happened to be—killed there tonight, England, tomorrow, would have a new king . . .

BLACK BISHOP (reacts violently):

>But that's murder! I'll have nothing to do— ·

SIR GUY (quiet menace):

>You'll do what you're told to do—and that's very simple. Keep your mouth closed!

BLACK BISHOP (to Prince John):

>Your Highness, I—I beg you not to—

PRINCE JOHN (coldly):

>How long will you retain your abbey if Richard survives to find out what you've been up to, these years he's been away? (To Sir Guy.) Go on, Gisbourne . . . Who's to—

SIR GUY:

>Dispose of Richard? (Jerks head toward Dickon.) Dickon was a knight, till your brother hacked off his spurs over some little mischance. (Smiles.) There's nothing he wouldn't do for a king who'd restore him to rank.[23]

181

He turns and motions Dickon to approach. Marian, by now, is halfway down the stairway, listening in horror.

PRINCE JOHN (to Dickon):
> You don't love my brother, I hear?

DICKON (sullenly):
> I've little reason to—sire!

PRINCE JOHN (pleased):
> You know this tavern?

DICKON:
> Yes.

343.   CLOSE SHOT   MARIAN   LISTENING ON STAIRWAY
standing flat against the pillar, frozen with incredulous horror. Prince John, Sir Guy, the Black Bishop, and Dickon in a group in the corridor below.

PRINCE JOHN:
> If Richard dies tonight . . .

He pauses. Sir Guy cuts eagerly in.

SIR GUY:
> . . . Sir Dickon Malbete reappears on the roll of English knights. Is that right, Your Highness?

PRINCE JOHN:
> Yes. With the manor and estates of Robin of Locksley to support his rank.

DICKON (instantly):
> When do I start, sire?

344.   MED. CLOSE SHOT   THE GROUP

PRINCE JOHN:
> At once! How many men will you need?

DICKON:
> None, sire! I'll do it better alone.

The others exchange understanding smiles. Dickon salutes and exits quickly out of scene. The others turn to watch him go, then look at each other. In background Marian starts again to descend the circular stairway around the pillar. They do not see her.

SIR GUY (to Prince John):
　　The sooner you assume the throne the less chance there'll be of trouble or uprising . . . (smiles sardonically) sire!

PRINCE JOHN (smiles):
　　You're a clever fellow, Gisbourne. (To Black Bishop.) Return to your abbey and make preparations to proclaim me king, here in Nottingham, the day after tomor—[24]

He breaks off suddenly, and stares, off. The others follow his gaze.

345.　　MED. SHOT　MARIAN
　　SHOOTING past the three, as she exits along the corridor. They turn back to each other, perplexed and alarmed.

BLACK BISHOP:
　　Do you suppose she . . .

Sir Guy and Prince John look at each other guardedly.

SIR GUY:
　　I don't know . . . but after I've seen Your Grace away, I'll find out.

The Black Bishop bows to Prince John and with Sir Guy exits. As Prince John looks after them,

DISSOLVE TO:

346.　　CLOSE SHOT　BESS　IN MARIAN'S CHAMBER　　NIGHT
She is worried, alert.

MARIAN'S VOICE (urgent):
> . . . and now you know why Robin's got to find King Richard at once, and warn him.

CAMERA PULLS BACK TO:

347. MED. SHOT   INT. MARIAN'S CHAMBER   NIGHT
Marian is at a desk, writing frantically, Bess watching her with tense concern.

MARIAN:
> Take this note to Much at the Saracen's Head . . .

She is interrupted by a knock at the door. The two stiffen in apprehension and exchange frightened glances. Marian waves Bess toward an adjoining room, and Bess swiftly exits. Marian attempts to hide her note and writing materials. There is another sharp rap; then, as Marian thrusts the note hastily under a cloth on the table, the door opens and Sir Guy enters and sees it. But he gives no sign. Marian gets up and faces him.

SIR GUY (smoothly):
> My lady's hearing is defective tonight?

Marian's control breaks in nervous, impetuous anger.

MARIAN:
> When you knock at a lady's door as though it were a tavern, you deserve to wait!

As he advances on her,

CAMERA MOVES UP TO:

348. TWO SHOT   MARIAN AND SIR GUY
He is cold, sure of himself. She is nervous and apprehensive.

SIR GUY:
> You seem upset.

MARIAN:
> Upset? Why should I . . .

SIR GUY:

Come now, my dear. You've played the innocent
long enough. Let's be frank with one another.

MARIAN:

I don't see the need for—

SIR GUY:

—for discussion? (Laughs.) You're charming,
Marian, but hardly clever. For instance, you couldn't
possibly have failed to overhear what we were talking about in the corridor just now—no-no!—(checks
her interruption) don't trouble to deny it! And your
first thought, as Richard's loyal ward, was to warn
him. Right?

Marian does not answer. Sir Guy now, while talking,
moves about the room, picking up and casually examining small objects, playing with her, CAMERA PANNING
with him, while she, like a bird caught in the deadly
fascination of a snake, watches him with dilated eyes.

SIR GUY:

Come, my dear—aren't I right?

MARIAN (lips trembling):

How could *I* warn Richard?

SIR GUY (sardonically):

How did Locksley and his men arrange his escape
from hanging after the archery match? *Someone* in
the castle here got him word . . .

MARIAN (vehemently):

That's ridiculous!

SIR GUY (approaches her, smiles thinly):

You think I've not noticed how your eyes glow when
Robin's name comes up . . . and how, in spite of
your pretended indifference, you've defended him.
(Again she would interrupt, but he shakes his head.)
I was afraid you'd notice how deliberately I intro-

185

duced those discussions . . . but your ardent re-
sponse never varied.

MARIAN (curtly):
Now you *are* being silly!

SIR GUY (disregards this; his voice becomes metallic):
But when I found that such tender interludes in-
duced in you a growing distaste for myself, it ceased
to be amusing.

MARIAN:
If that's all you have to say—

SIR GUY:
Not quite all. For when Richard's in danger, what
more natural than that you'd try to warn him
through Locksley? And you *do* intend to warn him,
don't you?

349. CLOSE SHOT   BESS
cowering terrified, and listening, in adjoining room.

SIR GUY'S VOICE (insistent):
Don't you?

MARIAN'S VOICE (desperate denial):
No!

350. MED. CLOSE SHOT   MARIAN AND SIR GUY
He moves casually toward her writing table.

SIR GUY (softly):
If that is true . . . (calmly takes her note to Robin
from beneath papers on table and reads it, then
looks up) perhaps you'll explain before Prince John
and the execution court the meaning—(holds up
note) of this!

Marian, in terrified reaction, tries to seize the note, but
he holds her off and shouts.

SIR GUY:
> *Guards!*

The door opens and four men-at-arms enter.

SIR GUY:
> Take my lady to the Great Hall.

As the men-at-arms escort Marian out, followed by Sir Guy, and the door closes, Bess emerges from the other room. She is terribly wrought up, does not know what to do. Paces, wringing her hands. Then, with sudden decision, she exits.

                                                    DISSOLVE TO:

351.   MED. FULL SHOT   NIGHT
        GREAT HALL OF NOTTINGHAM CASTLE
        Marian defiantly is facing Prince John who sits at a table, flanked by the high sheriff, Sir Mortimer, Sir Ralf, Sir Geoffrey, and three or four other Norman knights. Marian is speaking defiantly.

MARIAN:
> You ask me if I'm not ashamed! I am—bitterly! But it's a shame that I'm a Norman after seeing the things my fellow countrymen have done to England.

                                            CAMERA MOVES UP TO:

352.   MED. CLOSE SHOT   MARIAN
        as she continues defiantly.

MARIAN (continuing):
> At first I wouldn't believe! Because *I* was a Norman I wouldn't *let* myself believe that the horrors you inflicted on the Saxons weren't just and right! (To them all.) But I thank God my eyes were opened . . .

353.   CLOSE SHOT   PRINCE JOHN, SIR GUY, HIGH SHERIFF, KNIGHTS
        as they listen. Prince John's face is white with rage.

MARIAN'S VOICE (vibrant):
> I know now why you tried so hard to kill this outlaw you despised . . . It's because he was the one man in England who protected the helpless against a lot of beasts who were drunk on human blood!

354. MED. SHOT THE GROUP

MARIAN (to Prince John, passionate revulsion, emphasizing each word):
> And now you intend to murder your own brother!

PRINCE JOHN (harshly):
> You'll be sorry you interfered!

MARIAN:
> Sorry? I'd do it again—if you killed me for it!

PRINCE JOHN:
> A prophetic speech, my lady . . . for that is exactly what is going to happen to you.

MARIAN (turns to others):
> I am a royal ward of King Richard—and no one but the king himself has the right to condemn me to death!

PRINCE JOHN:
> You are quite right, my dear . . . (significantly) and it *shall* be a king, who will order your execution for high treason, exactly forty-eight hours from now.

He gestures to the guards to remove her, and she is led out.

DISSOLVE TO:

355. MED. SHOT INT. SARACEN'S HEAD NIGHT
Bess, in a turmoil, is facing Much. Humility Prin stands by. They are tense, terribly worried.

BESS (urgent, close to tears):
> And tell 'im my lady's been condemned to death. Got it all in yer stupid 'ead now? (Much nods.) Well,

give Robin the 'ole message exactly like I told it to
yer!

MUCH (terrific urgency):
Bess—where was Dickon to find Richard?

BESS (sobbing):
Never mind *'im!* Wot do I care for yer kings and
thrones and such? Robin's got to do something to
save my baby!

Much looks despairingly at Prin. The latter pats Bess on
the shoulder.

PRIN (coaxing):
Come on, old girl, Robin'll look after her all right.
Where's Dickon headin' for?

BESS:
The Kent Road Tavern.

The two men exchange quick, determined glances.

PRIN (low and quick, to Much):
You'll save three mile and cut him off, through Low
Wood.

Much nods. Together he and Prin roll the great cask from
the trapdoor in the floor and raise the door. Much runs
across to Bess.

MUCH (tenderly):
Kiss me, and wish me luck, lass!

BESS (impatient):
'Urry up! Take yer hugly face out of 'ere! (Gives him
a hasty kiss and shove. Much runs for the trapdoor
and starts down.) Be—be careful, Much . . . !

As he disappears and Prin closes the trapdoor,

DISSOLVE TO:

356.   MED. SHOT   MOONLIGHT[25]
FORD ACROSS STREAM IN FOREST
Dickon gallops into scene, pulls up in the middle of the

ford, and releases the reins so his horse can drink. (Spot at Chico for this.) Beyond Dickon, Much rises from a bush like a sinister shadow and darts out into the stream. Dickon hears the splash and whirls, then snatches his horse's head up and starts off; but Much, leaping after him, drags him from the saddle at the farther bank. The horse gallops on. As Much and Dickon fight with knives—a terrible, silent encounter in the moonlight, broken only by their hoarse panting and grunts as they roll over and over,

CAMERA MOVES UP TO:

357.   TWO SHOT   MUCH AND DICKON   NIGHT
in their fight to the death, as they roll over and over, half on the bank, half in the stream, their knives glinting in the moonlight. They rise, locked in each other's arms, struggling and slashing. Much is wounded, and it looks as if Dickon will finish him. They go into another flurry of blows, and each blade sinks home. Dickon crashes with Much on top. Then, as the body of his enemy lies still, Much staggers to his feet, stumbles, falls, picks himself up again, stands swaying over Dickon, then turns and plunges in a dreadful staggering run, badly hurt, into the forest.

FADE OUT

FADE IN

358.   FULL SHOT   ROAD IN SHERWOOD FOREST   DAY
An abbot with four of his monks (King Richard the Lion-Heart and his nobles in disguise) are riding leisurely along. With them are a number of sumpter horses heaped with baggage, linens, silverware, etc., giving the appearance of the chief of a great religious house traveling to visit the branches of his order.

359.   MED. SHOT   CURVE IN THE ROAD   DAY
Robin Hood jumps from the shrubbery into the road and stands waiting. The monastic party comes around

the turn. Robin holds up his hand, but Richard does not halt. He plods steadily forward and would run completely over Robin, except that he grasps the bridle of Richard's horse and so brings him to a halt.

ROBIN (wide smile):
> Greetings, Sir Abbot! You've traveled far, this morning?

RICHARD:
> Too far to be patient with delay now.

ROBIN:
> Perhaps it's the weight of your purse that wearies you so early in the day. Suppose you hand it to me. If it weighs more than a just amount, I'll share it with those who have less.

RICHARD:
> You think I hand my purse to every rough lout who asks for it?

Robin raises his bow at arm's length, and twenty of his green-clad outlaws jump into the road and cover the abbot's party with their arrows. Little John, Allan-a-Dale, and Friar Tuck are among them.

ROBIN (grinning deprecation):
> We're only poor outlaws, who have nothing to eat but the king's deer, while you have property, rents, and silver. So . . . (holds out his hand again) your purse.

360.   TWO SHOT   ROBIN AND RICHARD
Richard looks speculatively at Robin's men, then back at Robin.

RICHARD:
> But I've traveled far on the king's business, and the silver pennies I have left equal no more than sixty marks.

LITTLE JOHN (interjects quickly):
What—are you friendly to our King Richard?

RICHARD:
I love no man better!

ROBIN (quietly):
By that speech, Sir Abbot, you save half your money!
Give me only fifteen marks for the poor, and the rest
you may keep—and welcome.

RICHARD:
Then I'm free to go?

ROBIN:
Any friend of Richard is free of this forest . . . unless you'd honor me by sharing meat with me?

CAMERA PULLS BACK TO:

361.   MED. SHOT   ROBIN AND RICHARD
as Richard wheels and, with Robin walking at his side,
leads them off the road into the forest, CAMERA MOVING
with them.

RICHARD:
Gladly . . . ! But who are you?

ROBIN:
Robin Hood.

362.   MOVING TWO SHOT   ROBIN AND RICHARD
as they progress through the greenwood.

RICHARD (vaguely):
It seems I've heard the name . . .

ROBIN (grinning):
It *seems* you have? Why all England knows me!
(Amends.) The middle shires, anyway.

RICHARD (as one who suddenly recollects):
Ah—now I remember! But how does your loyalty

to Richard set on a killer of knights, a poacher of the king's deer and an outlaw?

ROBIN (his face grows serious):
Those I killed died because they'd misused the trust that Richard left them . . . and the worst rascal of the lot was the king's own brother.

RICHARD:
Then you blame Prince John?

ROBIN (vehemently):
No! I blame King Richard, whose job was here at home, protecting his people instead of deserting them to fight in foreign lands!

RICHARD (frowns):
What—you'd condemn the Holy Crusades?

ROBIN (stoutly):
I'd condemn anything that left the task of holding England for Richard to outlaws—like me!

Richard looks at him curiously, as they pass on.

DISSOLVE TO:

363. MED. CLOSE PAN SHOT   MUCH-THE-MILLER'S-SON
as he staggers, bleeding, ragged, exhausted, terribly hurt, through the forest undergrowth toward Robin's camp. He falls, gets up, falls again, and lies still. CAMERA PANS UP as Will Scarlet, on a horse, rides casually toward Much. Suddenly he sees him and rides forward, then swiftly dismounts, and turns Much over. He reacts, on recognizing him, with

WILL SCARLET:
Why, Much . . . ! What's happened to you, old fellow?

MUCH (revives slightly, hoarse gasp):
Take me to Robin . . . quick!

Will lifts him to his saddle, lies him across it, mounts, and gallops off in the direction in which Much was heading.

DISSOLVE TO:

364. ROBIN HOOD'S CAMP
Robin and his men, King Richard, and his retinue have just arrived at the camp, and from another direction Will Scarlet, holding the wounded Much, rides in.[26]

WILL'S VOICE:
Robin! Robin!

365. MED. LONG SHOT   WILL SCARLET   MOUNTED CARRYING MUCH
SHOOTING toward the rock steps at the edge of the camp, from Robin's angle, as the outlaws turn and stare. Will gallops down the steps into the camp and pulls up his horse. He leaps off and starts to lift Much off, but the latter, slumping half to the ground, sees Robin and, at the same time Robin starts toward him, staggers toward Robin at a shambling run. It is too much for him, however, and he topples forward on his face. Robin is followed by his outlaws, Richard, and his friends.

366. MED. CLOSE SHOT   MUCH
as he lies on the ground. Robin enters the shot and kneels, swiftly examining Much, then looks up at Will.

ROBIN (sharply):
Where'd you find him, Will?

WILL (jerks his head to forest):
Out there!

ROBIN (to his men):
Get some water! (To Much.) Much! What happened, friend?

Much does not answer; an outlaw enters the shot with

an earthen vessel containing water and a cloth. Robin rapidly sponges Much's face, and he begins feebly to revive. Will Scarlet kneels beside Robin and holds the vessel.

MUCH:
> Where's Robin . . . ?

ROBIN:
> I'm here, Much. What is it, old fellow? What happened?

MUCH (gasps, blood trickling from a corner of his mouth):
> King Richard's . . . in England . . .

WILL (exclaims incredulously):
> Wha-at?

Robin checks him with a quick glance and gesture and turns back to Much.

ROBIN:
> Go on, Much . . . ?

As Much speaks,

                              CAMERA PULLS BACK TO:

367.   MED. SHOT   THE GROUP
Richard and his friends listening, standing behind Robin.

MUCH:
> Prince John sent Dickon to . . . Kent Road Tavern last night . . . to kill the king . . .

Richard and his friends exchange startled glances. Robin turns to Will.

ROBIN (quick order):
> Will—take fifty men at once. Go to the Kent Road—

Much pulls Robin's arm, interrupting him.

MUCH:
> No need, master . . . I—I 'eaded Dickon off . . . 'E
> won't murder anybody—no more . . .

ROBIN:
> And the king? Where is he?

MUCH:
> I don't know, master.

ROBIN (grim):
> Men, we've got to find Richard—bring him here for
> safety at once. Little John! Take a party! Scour the
> countryside! Friar Tuck—go into the town! Will!
> Search every inn and cottage! Don't rest day or
> night, any of you, till Richard's found!

368. TWO SHOT   ROBIN AND RICHARD

RICHARD (a hand on Robin's arm):
> But you don't have to search for Richard, Robin.
> He's in good hands—the best in England.

Robin stares.

369. MED. SHOT   THE GROUP

All are staring at Richard, who stands now with his men
behind him. Richard's hand is at the fastening of his
cloak.

ROBIN:
> What do you mean? Where is he?

RICHARD (quietly):
> Here.

As he speaks, he unfastens his cloak, as do the others,
and all stand revealed in the magnificent armor of leading Crusaders. And on Richard's chest is emblazoned the
emblem of the king.[27] The crowd stands motionless in
thunderstruck silence.

370. CLOSE SHOT   ROBIN
as he stares an instant, unbelievingly at first, then with
devotion, affection, and happiness growing in his eyes.

ROBIN (almost reverently):
Sire!

He starts to kneel.

371. MED. SHOT   GROUP
As Robin kneels, bowing low before the king, others are
beginning to fully realize, and kneel.

372. MED. CLOSE SHOT   FRIAR TUCK, LITTLE JOHN, WILL
as they also, with happiness in their eyes, kneel and
bow.

373. FULL SHOT   GLADE
showing the entire band kneeling, bowed before the
stately figures of King Richard and his nobles.

374. CLOSE SHOT   RICHARD AND ESSEX
As Richard looks silently around at this large band of
devoted men, a strange gentle warmth and affection
comes into his eyes. He speaks slowly to Essex.

RICHARD:
All these . . . have remained loyal. (He smiles
down.) Rise . . . Sir Robin.

375. MED. SHOT   GROUP
As Robin rises, Richard speaks to the others.

RICHARD:
Rise . . . men of Sherwood.

As the band rises, Friar Tuck remains kneeling foreground. Richard looks at him.

FRIAR TUCK:

Sire . . . I'm only a poor curtal friar . . . and if I struck you—

RICHARD (smiles):

It was proof of the strength of a loyal arm. Rise, my friend.[28]

Friar Tuck's face lights with happiness, and he gets up. As he does so, his eyes catch those of Little John who is regarding him with a disgusted "fine-fool-you-were, hitting-the-king" expression. Friar Tuck's nose goes up in a ludicrously complacent and superior smirk.

376.   CLOSE SHOT   MUCH

MUCH:

Sire, Prince John's . . . calling Bishop o' . . . the Black Canons to proclaim 'im king in Nottingham tomorrow . . .

377.   GROUP SHOT

ROBIN:

How did you learn this?

MUCH:

Lady Marian . . . over'eard . . . They've took 'er for treason . . . She's been condemned . . . to the block . . . for warning us . . .

RICHARD:

He wouldn't dare to execute the king's ward.

ROBIN:

You underestimate him, sire. If we're to save Lady Marian and your throne, we've got to act *now*!

RICHARD:

How? By attacking the castle? (Shakes his head.)

Without an army it's much too strong. Your men would be killed uselessly.

ROBIN (thoughtfully):
If the Bishop of the Black Friars is going to the palace tomorrow to perform the ceremony—(looks at Richard and smiles significantly) suppose we visit him at the abbey tonight, and let *him* suggest a way.

As Richard looks at him, then, beginning to get the idea, smiles in grim approval,

FADE OUT

FADE IN

378. FULL SHOT   CAUSEWAY OF NOTTINGHAM CASTLE   DAY
NOTE: Over this sequence, SOUND TRACK carries the wild ringing of bells. This continues until the Black Bishop and his retinue enter the castle from the courtyard, or longer, at the discretion of the director.

The Bishop of the Black Canons and his long retinue of priests and monks cross the causeway, toward the castle courtyard portals. Ahead of the bishop are standard bearers carrying the religious insignia, a crucifix, etc. Next comes the Black Bishop, closely flanked by Richard in his abbot's dress. Behind them is a group of lesser church dignitaries—Richard's four nobles, including the earl of Essex, and Will Scarlet, Little John, Friar Tuck, and Allan-a-Dale, disguised as priests of the order of the Black Canons. Behind them is a long double or quadruple file of somber, hooded monks—Robin's outlaws, disguised as members of the Black Canons. All, except the Black Bishop, wear their cowls well forward over their faces. The illusion, to the audience, at first should be that this is a genuine procession of the bishop and his monks. The line moves forward with slow, impressive dignity, toward a large guard of honor of men-at-arms, who wait at the inner or castle end of the causeway.

379. CLOSE TRUCK SHOT   THE BLACK BISHOP

as he crosses the causeway. His face is serene, and he walks with calm, unhurried mien. After holding on the Black Bishop to establish his entire complacency, CAMERA DROPS SLOWLY BACK to include Robin and Richard, as they move forward, closely flanking the Black Bishop, whose face now becomes a little strained. The ensuing dialogue is delivered almost whispered and through barely moving lips.

ROBIN (grimly):
> Brace up! Smile . . . (the bishop's beam reappears) wider . . . (The smile enlarges.)

RICHARD:
> You're still sure it wasn't you who warned my brother I was in England?

BISHOP (acute distress):
> No, sire . . . ! I—it wasn't me! Believe me, I—

Robin prods him gently with a concealed knife, held at the Black Bishop's back.

ROBIN:
> Smile . . . !

The Black Bishop resumes his beneficent smile. CAMERA TRUCKS BACK to the group of church dignitaries—Little John, Friar Tuck, Will Scarlet, Allan-a-Dale, the earl of Essex, and Richard's other three nobles. Their faces are in the shadow of their hoods.

LITTLE JOHN (to Friar Tuck, mumbles):
> You'll sweat some of that lard off your carcass before this day's over, my pudgy friend.

FRIAR TUCK:
> I hope some Norman sword whittles you down to size!

CAMERA DROPS FURTHER BACK revealing the familiar faces of others of Robin's men.

380. MED. SHOT   DAY
     INT. PRINCE JOHN'S CHAMBER IN CASTLE
     Sir Guy is helping John to don a magnificent robe, while
     knights and nobles look on. These include Sir Ralf, Sir
     Geoffrey, and Sir Mortimer, in splendid court costumes.
     Prince John is in high good humor.

         PRINCE JOHN (low voice to Sir Guy):
             No news of Richard? (Sir Guy shakes his head.)
             Then Dickon must have . . .

     He leaves the sentence unfinished, and they exchange
     significant smiles.

381. FULL SHOT   CASTLE COURTYARD   DAY
     The head of the Black Bishop's procession has entered
     the castle, and the following lines of monks are disap-
     pearing through the door. The bells are ringing.

382. CLOSE SHOT   MARIAN   IN CELL
     standing beneath a narrow window, with a shaft of sun-
     light pouring down on her head. She is dressed as we
     last saw her (scene 354), and her hands are clasped over
     her ears in a despairing gesture, as though to shut out
     the torment of the clanging bells.

383. FULL SHOT   DAY
     INT. GREAT HALL OF NOTTINGHAM CASTLE
     On a dais is a large, thronelike chair under a canopy.
     The high sheriff, in dazzling robes of office, and looking
     most important, is in command of a heavy guard of
     men-at-arms. A gathering of Norman knights, ladies,
     and squires is present, all in full ceremonial court dress.
     The ladies are grouped at the end of the hall farthest
     from the dais, so when the battle starts they can flee
     through the doors, leaving the hall clear for the fight. A
     seneschal waits at the door, with two flanking lines of
     trumpeters. As the scene opens, the Black Bishop is

walking toward the dais, closely escorted by Robin, Richard, and their immediate friends. As they mount the dais, the lines of following monks split and range themselves before the men-at-arms who are in solid rank along the walls. Thus, the monks effectively cut off the dais from the protection of the Normans. The Black Bishop and his group on the dais turn toward the door.

384.   MED. CLOSE SHOT   LINE OF TRUMPETERS
as they raise their trumpets and blow a blast.

385.   MED. SHOT   THE GREAT HALL
SHOOTING from the dais toward the door as Prince John and his retinue enter from the corridor and proceed slowly toward the dais. Knights and squires bow, and ladies curtsy as he passes.

386.   MED. CLOSE SHOT   ROBIN, RICHARD, BISHOP, AND GROUP
as Prince John mounts the dais. Their heads turn to watch as CAMERA PANS with Prince John. The latter reaches the thronelike chair and sits down, his retinue grouped behind and to the side of him.

387.   TWO SHOT   ROBIN AND BLACK BISHOP
Robin nudges him to commence, and the bishop steps forward.

ROBIN:
    Remember . . . !

The bishop moves out of scene.

388.   MED. SHOT   DAIS
as the Black Bishop faces Prince John. Richard and his four nobles move ceremoniously after him, Robin and his friends remaining where they were. The faces of Richard and his friends are deep within their cowls.

389. MED. CLOSE SHOT   PRINCE JOHN, BLACK BISHOP, AND
RICHARD
The bishop forces himself to speak. He is tense, nervous.

BLACK BISHOP:
By what authority do you, John Lackland, Prince of
England, claim to be proclaimed this day, Sovereign
of the Realm, and, as Defender of the Holy Sepulchre, to receive the blessing of the church?

PRINCE JOHN (loudly):
By right of blood succession.

The Black Bishop hesitates, swallows, then turns back to
Richard as though to confer with him. Richard whispers
a few words. The Black Bishop turns back to John.

BLACK BISHOP:
Is it of your own free will that—(hesitates, shoots a
quick, panicky glance at Richard's face, stern within
its cowl) that you thus depose your brother, Richard
the Lion-Heart of England?

390. CLOSE SHOT   PRINCE JOHN
He stares in surprised anger at the Black Bishop.

PRINCE JOHN (harshly):
Richard no longer exists! From this moment forward I alone am king of England. He . . .

Suddenly he breaks off, his starting eyes fixed beyond
the Black Bishop.

RICHARD'S VOICE (cutting irony):
Aren't you a little premature, brother?

Off scene we hear the start of amazed tumult and exclamations of surprise and consternation.

391. FULL SHOT   RICHARD AND NOBLES
Their religious robes have been dropped, and they stand
forth in the magnificent and brilliantly emblazoned sur-

touts and chain mail of their station. The crowd's murmur grows to an excited roar that increases when suddenly, at a signal from Robin, the monks of the Black Canons drop their habits and reveal themselves in their outlaw costume of Lincoln green.

THE CROWD (ad lib):
Richard! The Lion-Heart! The king lives! Robin Hood! King Richard! It's the king! It is! It is! With the outlaws! Etc . . . etc . . .

The ensuing scenes break with explosive suddenness. Prince John, sick with fear, cringes back before Richard, but Sir Guy and his immediate friends, knowing their goose is cooked, make a last desperate bid. Guy looks around at them with blazing, reckless eyes and they close around him. Sir Guy's sword flashes out, and his friends and other Norman knights follow suit.

SIR GUY:
He's an imposter! Seize him! Kill him!

Sir Guy leaps forward at Richard and tries to cut him down. Robin leaps forward and parries the blow, trying to engage Sir Guy, but immediately the battle starts. The men-at-arms attack the outlaws, and in the general tumult and melee Robin and Sir Guy are swept apart. Richard and his friends force Prince John before them to the back of the dais and there prevent him from escape, although they are attacked by Norman knights and men-at-arms. The fight now is general.

392.   MED. FULL SHOT   END OF GREAT HALL
as a number of the outlaws herd the ladies through a door or preferably into a corner out of harm's way, then turn to meet and beat back an attack of the men-at-arms.

393.   MED. SHOT   THE BATTLE
as it rages all over the Great Hall and around the dais, which is like a besieged island, defended by the outlaws

against Sir Guy and his followers who are trying to get at Richard. The high sheriff dances, terrified, in background.

394. TWO SHOT   WILL SCARLET AND SIR MORTIMER
as they battle with swords. The battle is raging around them.

WILL SCARLET (almost bored):
Where will you have it? (Sir Mortimer feints and lunges but misses.) Lost your tongue? (Hacks Sir Mortimer down.) Well, you won't need it now.[29]

He turns back to the fight.

395. MED. SHOT   THE FIGHT
The Normans are being beaten back.

396. MED. CLOSE SHOT   ROBIN AND WILL SCARLET
in the battle. Will cuts down a knight and a man-at-arms, then, as Robin is engaged with another and is about to finish him, Will leaps in and does it for him. Robin flashes Will a grin.

ROBIN:
Don't be greedy!

As they fight.

397. MED. CLOSE SHOT   LITTLE JOHN AND FRIAR TUCK
battling against Sir Geoffrey, Sir Ralf, and others. Tuck is knocked off his feet. Sir Ralf, about to finish him, is killed by Little John, who now yells down at Friar Tuck.

LITTLE JOHN:
Do you have to sleep with this going on? (Kicks him in the ribs.) Get up, you lazy oaf!

Friar Tuck scrambles up and into the fight, sees Sir Mortimer about to cut down Little John from behind.

FRIAR TUCK (sharply, to Sir Mortimer, as to a naughty child):
Ah!-ah!-ah!

Sir Mortimer, startled, checks, and Friar Tuck, unable to reach that far, throws his sword. It catches Sir Mortimer like a thunderbolt and he drops. Friar Tuck snatches a sword from a man-at-arms.

FRIAR TUCK:
Give me that! Do you want to hurt yourself?

He gives the man a terrific kick which lays him out, then wades into the fight again, sword moving like a flail.

398. CLOSE SHOT ROBIN
near the door leading to corridor. In corridor, background, is a circular pillar with steps leading down, around it. Robin is battling an enormous man-at-arms and a Norman squire. He kills the squire, then whirls on the man-at-arms, beats him to his knees, and puts his sword to the man's throat.

ROBIN:
Where's the Lady Marian? *Quick!*

MAN-AT-ARMS (stammers):
Un-under the West Keep.

ROBIN:
Which way?

The man points to the stairway, leading down, and Robin, knocking the man out with a terrific swipe of the flat of his sword, makes for the stairway.

399. CLOSE SHOT SIR GUY FIGHTING
In the midst of the melee he sees Robin making for the stairway and immediately guesses his purpose. With sudden and ferocious excess of energy he beats his attackers down and breaks away, heading for Robin.

400. MED. SHOT   HEAD OF CIRCULAR STAIRWAY
Just as Robin reaches it Sir Guy leaps in front of him,
sword upraised. They immediately engage.
                                    CAMERA MOVES UP TO:

401. TWO SHOT   ROBIN AND SIR GUY FIGHTING
Robin parries a terrific slash.

ROBIN:
> Did I—(cut and parry) spoil your party?

SIR GUY (brilliant, savage attack):
> Not at all. I'm pleased—(presses him) at this chance
> to—(terrific stroke which Robin fends) meet you
> alone . . .

They are near the stair. Melee in background.

ROBIN:
> Indeed? (Fast cut and parry.) Then your actions have
> been singularly deceptive . . . (his sword flashes
> around his foe, driving him backward) for every
> time you've sought me . . . (terrific attack) you've
> taken good care to have plenty of company!

Sir Guy tries desperately to hold his ground, but Robin
forces him back near the steps, closely following him.
The motive in this fight is that Sir Guy tries to prevent
Robin from descending the stairway. In background, the
Normans are retreating, some running from the fight.

402. MED. CLOSE SHOT   THE DUEL
The faces of both men are running with sweat. Sir Guy's
face wears the wolfish grin of desperation. Robin is
grimly determined to finish him off.

ROBIN:
> Do you know—(hacking blow) any prayers, my
> friend?

SIR GUY (pants):
> I'll say some for you!

ROBIN:

> I'm afraid you'd send 'em in the wrong direction! That reminds me—(strike, feint, strike) where would you like—(parries attack) to be buried?

He is pressing Sir Guy close to the circular hole through which the steps descend, and their blades are locked. By sheer strength Robin is forcing him back when suddenly Sir Guy's knee comes up with excruciating force into Robin's groin. Robin's sword flies from his hand. Sir Guy raises his own sword, but Robin, summoning his facilities, dives under his guard and takes him by the throat. Sir Guy drops his sword. They battle, face close to face, smashing, grappling, choking. In background, the Normans are rapidly being beaten back.

ROBIN (gasps):

> You should be disqualified.

SIR GUY:

> All's fair . . .

ROBIN:

> I don't mean using your knee . . .

SIR GUY (pants):

> What, then?

ROBIN (grins):

> You've been eating . . . (throttles him) onions!

With savage fury Sir Guy butts him in the face. Robin staggers back. Sir Guy leaps for his sword, recovers it, and hurls himself at Robin. Robin sidesteps, and Sir Guy hurtles past him, crashes into the pillar, and falls headlong down the stairwell. Robin runs down after him.

403. MED. SHOT EXT. MARIAN'S CELL

Two men-at-arms and a turnkey are standing, swords out, staring along the corridor. Off scene there is the sound of Sir Guy's falling body. Two of the men immediately run toward the sound. The turnkey is about to follow, then, mindful of his duty, he glances at the cell door and remains on guard, with naked sword.

404.   MED. CLOSE SHOT   SIR GUY'S LIFELESS BODY
at the foot of the circular stair. His sword is shown below him as though it had pierced his body when he fell. Robin jumps from the stairs into the scene, glances at Sir Guy, then looks off as we hear the feet of the onrushing men-at-arms. Robin swiftly recovers Sir Guy's sword. The men-at-arms leap to the attack and they fight, over Sir Guy's body. Robin cuts them down and runs along the corridor, CAMERA PANNING with him.

405.   MED. CLOSE SHOT   EXT. MARIAN'S CELL
as Robin runs up the turnkey throws down his sword.

TURNKEY:
    Robin . . . ! (In terror.) Have mercy, good master! I
    didn't know . . .

ROBIN:
    Open that door!

The turnkey's trembling hands fumble at the lock. Robin snatches the key and unlocks the door.

406.   MED. SHOT   INT. MARIAN'S CELL
SHOOTING PAST her to the door as it opens and Robin enters.

MARIAN:
    Robin . . . !

He sweeps her into his arms.

ROBIN:
    Are you all right, darling?

MARIAN:
    Oh, yes! How—what happened?

ROBIN:
> We've taken the castle. Richard's with us!

MARIAN (overjoyed):
> Richard safe? Oh . . . !

ROBIN:
> Yes, Quick now . . . come with me! I've got to join him![30]

DISSOLVE TO:

407.   MED. FULL SHOT   RICHARD AND PRINCE JOHN

in the Great Hall. The fighting is over, and John stands on the dais with his sullen, defeated Norman survivors held back by a press of triumphant outlaws. Richard faces Prince John. Richard's nobles, Robin and his friends, Marian, and the craven, dejected Bishop of the Black Canons, as well as the terrified high sheriff, the latter in the grip of Friar Tuck and Little John, stand just behind Richard. The women have reentered the hall and stand in background. The face of Richard is like the throne of Judgment. Prince John's is livid with fear and humiliation.

CAMERA MOVES UP TO:

408.   MED. CLOSE SHOT   THE GROUP AT DAIS

PRINCE JOHN (terrible shock):
> Richard! Richard—I—I thought—

RICHARD (sternly):
> You thought I was safely murdered.

PRINCE JOHN:
> No-no! Forgive me, Richard! I—I didn't mean to—
> I—After all, I *am* your brother . . .

RICHARD:
> I could forgive you if your treachery had been only against me, and not against my subjects. (Looks around at Prince John's knights.) I banish you and

your knights from England for the remainder of my
lifetime . . . [31] (pause) and I pray only that I may have
a son to succeed to my throne . . . ! (His gesture is
almost weary; to Essex.) Take them away, Essex. See
that they leave the country.

Prince John directs at Richard a look of malevolent hatred.
Essex touches his arm and he leaves, followed by his
friends. Richard watches them go, then turns to Robin.
As he begins to speak, SOUND TRACK carries once more
the sound of joyous clanging of bells, and from a distance comes the enthusiastic roar of the people in the
courtyard outside.

RICHARD (to Robin, somberly):
And what about you? Is there nothing England's
king can grant the outlaw who taught him his duty
to his country?

ROBIN:
Yes, sire . . . ! A free pardon for all my men.

RICHARD:
Granted, with all my heart! But—(glances at Marian)
is there nothing for yourself?

ROBIN (smiles):
I see Your Majesty has guessed—

RICHARD (to Marian):
And do you, too, wish—

MARIAN (low tone; glance at Robin):
More than anything in the world, sire . . .

RICHARD:
Kneel, Robin Hood . . .

409.   TWO SHOT   ROBIN AND RICHARD
as Robin drops to his knees. Richard lays his sword
blade on each shoulder in turn.

RICHARD:

Arise, Robin, baron of Locksley, earl of Sherwood and Nottingham, and lord of all the lands and manors appertaining thereto . . . (Robin rises, eyes shining. In background Marian's face is radiant.) My first command to you, my lord earl . . .

As Richard speaks CAMERA PULLS SLOWLY BACK, and the bells off scene break out in triumphant clamor.

RICHARD (continuing):

. . . is to take in marriage—(Richard places Marian's hand in Robin's) the hand of my dear ward, the Lady Marian Fitzwalter.

Robin's outlaws raise a terrific cheer. The bells ring out.

410. TWO SHOT ROBIN AND MARIAN
Richard, outlaws, etc., smiling in background.

ROBIN (to Richard):

May I obey all of Your Majesty's commands with equal pleasure!

He turns to Marian and kisses her, folding her in his arms. As the cheers of those present and the joyous ringing of the bells blend with the upward and triumphant surge of the background music,

FADE OUT

THE END

Annotation to the Screenplay

Although the script is dated September 25, 1937, and marked "Fourth Revised Final," it does contain changes (without the dates of the changes) that were made later, but before photography of the modified scenes. Also, in some cases, the script reflects added scenes and retakes that were being written throughout the filming and as late as January 5, 1938—near the end of production. The screenplay is "as written," however, not "as filmed," so that one is able to analyze the evolution from script to edited film.

1 The historical information in the titles is not entirely accurate. Richard left England for France in December 1189 and then set out in the summer of 1190 for the Holy Land. Before leaving, he divided the government of England between two justiciars: Hugh Puiset, bishop of Durham, in the north, and William Longchamp, chancellor and bishop of Ely, in the south. Longchamp, a Norman who despised Englishmen, got rid of Puiset and took over completely. He has been described as being exceptionally pompous and overbearing, and his tactless and autocratic methods eventually brought about his downfall.

2 The word "king" was deleted in the final edit. Leopold of Austria was Duke Leopold. Richard was seized near Vienna toward the end of December 1192.

3 Scene 6 either was not filmed or was eliminated while the film was being edited.

4 Since Warners' agreement with MGM prohibited singing of any kind (see page 18), this was deleted.

5 The original ransom demand was fixed at 100,000 marks, but several months later, in July of 1193, it was raised to 150,000 marks.

6 In October of 1191, the prelates, barons, and burghers confirmed the deposition of Longchamp and proclaimed Walter of Coutances chief justiciar; however, John was recognized as heir to the throne if Richard failed to return.

7 The remainder of scene 71 was deleted.

8 Changed to DAY.

9 The remainder of scene 116 and scenes 117, 118, and 119 were apparently photographed but later cut.

10 Scene 122 is not in the film.

11 Bess, Lady Marian's maid-in-waiting, does not derive from the Robin Hood tradition, but she was a character in Rowland Leigh's first draft continuity.

12 The word *night* was inadvertently retained from an earlier draft. The sequence played in the daytime.

13 Scenes 163, 165, 167, 168, 170, 171, and 172 are not in the film. Scenes 164, 166, and 169 remain.

14 The preceding sequence is very close to one in Rowland Leigh's early draft, except that Sir Guy, in Leigh's version, has the idea for the archery tournament.

15 The structure of the archery tournament sequence was different in some respects in the version that was photographed originally.

16 The first portion of scene 280 was not reshot, or, if it was, it was not used.

17 Scene 292 is extremely close to the one in Rowland Leigh's version, except that in the latter the sheriff addresses Robin and pronounces sentence.

18 Scene 297 was not shot.

19 Although photographed, scenes 316, 317, and 318 were later cut, and the sequence as it stands begins with scene 319.

20 Some of the dialogue between Robin and Marian on the following pages was pruned and slightly modified at the request of Errol Flynn. His changes stand in the film.

21 Scene 324 is not in the film.

22 Dürenstein, a fortress on a rock above the Danube where Richard had been kept prisoner.

23 Dickon Malbete does not derive from the Robin Hood tradition or history.

24 There were no preparations in Nottingham or anywhere else to proclaim John king at this time.

25 Changed to DAYLIGHT.

26 Just before the entrance of Will and Much, a rather lengthy scene had been written and, based on the evidence of still photographs, at least partially filmed. It dealt with archery practice in Robin's camp, followed by Richard, still in disguise, and Friar Tuck exchanging blows with their fists after the Friar had been challenged in sport by Richard (figure 15). The king proves his mettle and is about to take on Robin when Will rides in with Much.

27 The studio received a considerable amount of mail complaining about the appearance of crosses on the chests of Richard's Crusaders. Knights of the Crusades wore crosses on their chests while leav-

ing for the Holy Land and on their backs upon returning. The license was a deliberate one in order to make the revealment of the king and his nobles more effective dramatically.

28 Friar Tuck's and Richard's dialogue was in reference to the material described in note 26. These lines were cut, as well as the business between Little John and Friar Tuck.

29 All of the dialogue during the battle, with the exception of two sets of exchanges between Robin and Sir Guy during the duel, was eliminated.

30 All of the dialogue in scene 406 was deleted.

31 John was in France or Normandy at the time of Richard's return to England. The governing council of England unanimously decreed that John should be deprived of all of his lands in England, and that his castles should be seized because of his treasonable designs. Later, somewhere in Normandy, John and Richard were reconciled through the intervention of their elderly mother, Eleanor of Aquitaine (a character eliminated from all of the Robin Hood feature films with the exception of Disney's 1952 live-action version).

Production Credits

Executive Producer	Hal B. Wallis
Associate Producer	Henry Blanke
Directed by	Michael Curtiz and William Keighley
Screenplay by	Norman Reilly Raine and Seton I. Miller
Music composed and conducted by	Erich Wolfgang Korngold
Dialogue Director	Irving Rapper
Second Unit Director	B. Reeves Eason
Photography by	Tony Gaudio A.S.C. and Sol Polito A.S.C.
Film Editor	Ralph Dawson
Art Director	Carl Jules Weyl
Costumes by	Milo Anderson
Make-up Artist	Perc Westmore
Sound by	C. A. Riggs
Photographic Representative: Technicolor Corporation	W. Howard Greene
Technicolor Color Director	Natalie Kalmus
Associate	Morgan Padelford
Technical Adviser	Louis Van Den Ecker
Orchestrations	Hugo Friedhofer and Milan Roder
Musical Director	Leo F. Forbstein
Unit Production Manager	Al Alleborn
Archery Supervisor	Howard Hill
Fencing Master	Fred Cavens
Assistant Directors	Lee Katz and Jack Sullivan

Running time: 102 minutes
Released: May 1938

Cast

Robin Hood	Errol Flynn
Maid Marian	Olivia de Havilland
Sir Guy of Gisbourne	Basil Rathbone
Prince John	Claude Rains
Will Scarlet	Patric Knowles
Friar Tuck	Eugene Pallette
Little John	Alan Hale
High Sheriff of Nottingham	Melville Cooper
King Richard the Lion-Heart	Ian Hunter
Bess	Una O'Connor
Much-the-Miller's-Son	Herbert Mundin
Bishop of the Black Canons	Montagu Love
Sir Essex	Leonard Willey
Sir Ralf	Robert Noble
Sir Mortimer	Kenneth Hunter
Sir Geoffrey	Robert Warwick
Sir Baldwin	Colin Kenny
Sir Ivor	Lester Matthews
Dickon Malbete	Harry Cording
Captain of archers	Howard Hill
Proprietor of Kent Road Tavern	Ivan Simpson
Crippen	Charles McNaughton
Humility Prin	Lionel Belmore
Sir Nigel	Austin Fairman
Sir Norbert	Crauford Kent
Herald at archery tournament	Reginald Sheffield
Archery official	Wilfred Lucas
Archery referee	Holmes Herbert
Phillip of Arras	James Baker

Appendix

The Jousting Tournament

The jousting tournament, from the "Revised Final" screenplay of September 14, 1937, was eliminated from the script during the first week of production—long before it was scheduled to be filmed. Because it was planned as a spectacular opening sequence (see pages 23–24), it is important in the evolution of the screenplay.

FADE IN

1.　　CLOSE SHOT　FLUTTERING BANNER　　　　　　DAY
containing the brilliantly colored royal arms of Richard the Lion-Heart, king of England. SUPERIMPOSED on this is the following title:

ENGLAND—1193

When Richard the Lion-Heart, king of England, left for the Crusades in 1191, he put England under a regency, not trusting his treacherous, Saxon-hating brother, Prince John.

As the title continues, Richard's banner in background.

DISSOLVES TO:

2.　　CLOSE SHOT　FLUTTERING BANNER　　　　　　DAY
containing the arms of Prince John. The SUPERIMPOSED title continues:

Bitterly resentful, and backed by powerful Norman barons, Prince John avidly watched for an excuse to seize the regents' power, amusing himself, meanwhile, with minor oppressions of the Saxons and the pleasures of the hunt and the joust.

DISSOLVE TO:

3.   MED. SHOT   THE JOUSTING LISTS   DAY
in Nottingham Castle courtyard. A great concourse of
knights, ladies, and people, with brightly striped pavil-
ions, waving pennons, etc., the blazing silks and velvets
of the nobility contrasting with the more sober garb of
the people and the rags and dirt of beggars and serfs.
There are mounted heralds, announcing and keeping
score of the combats; the squires of competing knights
to replace broken lances, lead off weary or wounded
horses, provide portions of damaged armor, etc.; and,
posted everywhere outside the lists, a number of jongleurs, or wandering minstrels, who celebrate, with noisy
flourishes, each feat of arms and every fortunate or brilliant stroke. In the center box are Prince John, Lady
Marian Fitzwalter, and a number of Norman and Saxon
knights and ladies. The Normans are the favored ones,
clustered close around the prince, who has Marian at his
side. The Saxon spectators generally are more poorly
dressed and inferior in spirit to the Normans. Mainly,
Saxon and Norman spectators remain at the side from
which their respective champions enter. The lists are a
space in the courtyard before the royal box, sixty paces
long and forty paces broad. Down the center, longitudi-
nally, is a brightly painted wooden barrier, about two
feet high, to keep separate the jousting knights, while at
each end of the lists are barred gates high enough to
prevent the horses jumping over them at the end of their
run. The jousting lances carry metal coronels on their
ends.

As we open on this scene the crowd is stilled, while
two knights in full armor, visors down and the favors of
their ladies fluttering from their helmets, riding at full
gallop, meet with terrific force and the splintering of
lances in the center of the lists. Both knights crash out of
the saddles and a horse goes down in a cloud of dust.
There is a scream of excitement from the crowd, and

squires run forward to assist the fallen knights to their feet.

4.   MED. CLOSE SHOT   MOUNTED HERALD
with a scoring sheet in his hand, as he looks toward the fallen knights. He looks down to his score sheet and writes.

5.   CLOSE SHOT   JOUSTING SCORE SHEET
(See *Encyclopaedia Britannica*, 11th ed. [s.v. "Heraldry"], plate IV. Raine has this edition in his office if not available at Research.)
The sheet contains the names:

> du Lac
> Jernyngham
>
> Le Rochepot
> Lancaster
>
> de Crecy
> Montagu
>
> St. Bryce
> Momorancy
>
> Le Grimme
> Beaumont
>
> Gisbourne
> Locksley

The first name of each pair is a Norman, the other a Saxon. All have been scored, except the last two, and the Normans are overwhelmingly victorious in the scores. The herald's hand comes into the shot and puts the final victorious stroke on le Grimme's score. Gisbourne and Locksley's scores still are blank.

6.   MED. CLOSE SHOT   MOUNTED HERALD
as he looks up from his score and blows his trumpet. Silence.

HERALD (shouts):
> The winner of the last joust, on points, is that gallant Norman knight . . . Sir Geoffrey le Grimme!

There is tremendous applause from the Normans present.

7.   MED. SHOT   THE LISTS
yelling and cheering the victor. Both knights are being helped away, and the fallen horse is being dragged off. Down at the Saxon end of the field there is strained, unhappy silence.

8.   MED. SHOT   GROUP OF SAXONS
with glum, set faces. They are poorly dressed and dispirited. Men, women, and children, and a withered old grandmother.

OLD SAXON:
> Seems like nothing's gone right with us Saxons— not even sport—since Richard went to the Crusades.

YOUNG SAXON:
> And that's why, father! The king took the best of our Saxon knights with him—

SAXON WOMAN:
> —and them that's left hasn't money enough for decent horse flesh, time Prince John and his Norman friends gets through cheating 'em of all they own. Look at him over there, gloating . . .

They look across.

9.   MED. SHOT   THE ROYAL BOX
Prince John and his friends are jubilant, and Marian and the ladies are all smiles.

                                        CAMERA MOVES UP TO:
10.   MED. CLOSE SHOT   PRINCE JOHN'S PARTY
as they clap and applaud, with ad lib admiring comments to each other.

PRINCE JOHN (to Marian):
> Well, my Lady Marian . . . was it worth coming
> with me from London, to see what stout arms our
> Nottingham friends have? (Marian nods, smiling,
> and Prince John turns to a knight behind him.)
> Who's next?

Before the man can answer the herald's trumpet blows,
and they turn to look.

11.   MED. CLOSE SHOT   HERALD
as he lowers his trumpet.

HERALD (shouts):
> The next joust will be between that valiant Norman
> knight, lord of the Castle of Nottingham and the
> Midland shires . . .

WIPE OFF TO:

12.   MED. CLOSE SHOT   SIR GUY OF GISBOURNE
as he sits his horse, in full armor except for his helmet,
which is carried by his mounted squire behind him.

HERALD'S VOICE:
> . . . Sir Guy of Gisbourne!

SOUND TRACK carries the frenzied applause of the Normans in the crowd. A blast of the herald's horn brings
silence.

HERALD'S VOICE:
> . . . and the Saxon knight—

13.   MED. CLOSE SHOT   SIR ROBIN OF LOCKSLEY (ROBIN
HOOD)
as he sits his horse in full armor, with lance, sword, and
shield, the latter bearing his device—black arrows on a
field of white. His helmet is carried by his squire, Will
of Gamwell (Will Scarlet). Standing at the bridle of Robin's horse is his groom, Much-the-Miller's-Son, a serf.

HERALD'S VOICE:

   . . . Sir Robin of Locksley!

There is tremendous cheering from the Saxons. Robin looks down at Much and winks. Much winks back and grins, delighted.

14.   MED. SHOT THE SAXON CROWD
as they whoop and cheer. Tumblers turn handsprings. Jongleurs strike their harps. Robin, smiling, in background.

SAXON WOMAN (calls):

   Bless ye, Sir Robin! Go in and win for us.

SAXON MAN (to another):

   This won't be the first blow he's struck for us Saxons!

The herald's trumpet sounds again, and Robin, followed by Will, CAMERA PANNING with them, rides toward the center of the lists to meet Sir Guy, who is riding in from the opposite side. They meet together in the center, wheel, and ride abreast, followed by their squires, toward the royal box. The Saxons yell their approbation, above the cheers of the Normans.

15.   MED. CLOSE SHOT PRINCE JOHN'S GROUP
SHOOTING toward Robin and Sir Guy as they ride toward the box.

MARIAN (to Prince John):

   This Saxon seems to have many friends, Your Highness.

PRINCE JOHN:

   A lot of good they'll do him against Gisbourne. (Turns to group of Norman knights.) Who is this Robin of Locksley?

SIR IVOR LE NOIR (angrily):

   He's a troublemaker, Prince John.

PRINCE JOHN:
Trouble—?

SIR GEOFFREY LE GRIMME:
Yes, sire! An impudent, reckless rogue, who goes about the shire stirring up the Saxons against authority.

PRINCE JOHN:
You mean—he defies the Crown?

SIR GEOFFREY (indignantly):
Not only defies it, but sets himself up as a savior of the people!

PRINCE JOHN:
Indeed . . . (peers forward) I must bear him in mind! (Smiles thinly.) Meanwhile Sir Guy'll cut his comb today . . . ! Eh, Marian?

But Marian, her eyes fixed on the approaching knights, does not hear.

16.   TRUCK SHOT   ROBIN AND SIR GUY
as they ride toward the royal box, followed by their squires.

ROBIN (sideways to Sir Guy, cheerfully):
You're looking uncommonly pleased with yourself, Sir Guy. Planning a hanging or two?

SIR GUY (quiet venom):
I know a fit subject for one.

ROBIN (grins):
You might have more luck with a rope than you'll have with your lance.

Sir Guy directs toward his serenely impudent face a look of hatred.

17.   TWO SHOT   PRINCE JOHN AND MARIAN
as Robin and Sir Guy approach.

PRINCE JOHN:
    The Saxon's a handsome dog—eh, Marian?

MARIAN (looks at approaching knights, coolly):
    Sir Guy pleases me better.

PRINCE JOHN:
    Ah—then you *do* like him? I thought—

MARIAN:
    He's a Norman, sire!

PRINCE JOHN:
    Is that the only reason?

MARIAN:
    Reason enough, for a royal ward who must obey
    her guardian!

PRINCE JOHN:
    Nay—I'd not force you, my lady . . .

18.   MED. CLOSE PAN SHOT   ROBIN AND SIR GUY
as they ride up to the royal box, halt, and salute with
lances held high. As CAMERA PANS to their halt it brings
Marian and Prince John into shot. Prince John is still
speaking.

PRINCE JOHN:
    You may like whom you please . . . (sly, teasing hu-
    mor) even the Saxon.

Robin bows to her. Marian gives him a freezing glance.

MARIAN (cold arrogance):
    I prefer Sir Guy.

She smiles at Sir Guy, who gives a pleased bow. Robin
watches her with sardonic amusement. Prince John raises
his arm to the herald, off scene.

19.   CLOSE SHOT - THE HERALD

HERALD (shouts):
Know ye, good people, that in this, the final joust of
the day, according to ancient custom the visiting
knight shall have the right, if he so desire, to demand of the Lady Marian Fitzwalter, our maid of
honor, or whomsoever else he deem the fairest, her
favor, to wear as a gage, into the combat.

20.   MED. SHOT   GROUP AT ROYAL BOX
Marian, who has taken her kerchief and is about to
hand it to Sir Guy, pauses, astonished and angry.

MARIAN (indignantly, to Prince John):
Does that mean, Your Highness, I am to give it . . .
(glares at Robin) to the *Saxon?*

ROBIN (instantly and suavely):
My lady did not hear well. The herald said: "whom-
soever I deem the fairest . . . " (To Prince John.)
Does that mean I make my own choice, sire?

Puzzled, Prince John nods. Robin slowly, ignoring
Marian, looks over the other Norman beauties, then
turns his horse and walks along the front of the box, all
heads turning to watch him. He is followed by Will of
Gamwell.

21.   MED. SHOT   NORMAN LADIES IN ROYAL PAVILION
looking toward Robin as he rides toward them, followed
by Will. Some look disdainful, others hopeful, others
simpering, but Robin, ignoring them all, rides coolly
past, CAMERA PANNING with him, toward a group of
Saxons of the poorest sort. The Norman women stare,
indignant and mortified.

22.   MED. SHOT   GROUP OF SAXON SERFS
as Robin rides up. They are ragged and forlorn looking,
and among them is the withered old crone we saw in a

previous scene. Robin halts before her and salutes with
grave courtesy.

ROBIN (as though to a queen):
I beg your favor, my lady!

The old woman, confused and somewhat frightened,
backs away, but Robin leans close.

23.   TWO SHOT   ROBIN AND OLD SAXON WOMAN

ROBIN (urgent whisper and grin):
Hurry up, granny! Give me your kerchief! Anything! Quick!

The old woman's eyes glisten. Hastily she whips off her
kerchief, gives her nose a hasty rub with it, and hands it
to Robin, who bows low and kisses her hand. SOUND
TRACK carries the sudden tumultuous cheering and applause of the Saxon spectators.

24.   MED. SHOT   ROBIN
as he straightens, again salutes the old woman, then
canters rapidly back to the royal box, followed by Will.

25.   MED. SHOT   GROUP AT ROYAL BOX
as Robin canters back and takes his place alongside Sir
Guy. Marian, furious, and Prince John, his face dark
with fury, are standing. Marian still holds her kerchief.
As Robin returns, Marian furiously thrusts her kerchief
into Sir Guy's hand, but her angry eyes are on Robin,
who remains perfectly composed. Again both knights
raise their lances in salute, wheel about, and gallop away,
followed by their squires to their respective ends of the
lists.

26.   MED. CLOSE SHOT   SIR GUY
at the end of the lists, as his squire hands him his helmet. Sir Guy hastily ties on Marian's favor and puts on

the helmet, snapping down the visor. His lance comes down to rest.

27. CLOSE SHOT ROBIN
He ties on the old woman's favor and places the helmet on his head. He closes the visor and his lance comes to rest.

28. FULL SHOT THE TOURNAMENT
The herald's trumpet blows, and, amid the breathless hush of the crowd, Robin and Sir Guy start their gallop forward from the opposite ends of the lists.

29. MED. CLOSE DOLLY SHOT SIR GUY
as he gallops toward Robin.

30. MED. CLOSE DOLLY SHOT ROBIN
as he gallops toward Sir Guy.

31. MED. FULL SHOT ROBIN AND SIR GUY
They collide violently in the center of the lists. Both lances are splintered, but neither is unhorsed. SOUND TRACK carries a sudden yell of excitement from the crowd. As the knights wheel to return to the ends of the lists, their squires ride out and hand them fresh lances. The knights turn again and once more gallop toward each other.

32. MED. CLOSE SHOT ROBIN AND SIR GUY
as they meet with terrific force. Robin's lance catches Sir Guy squarely and hurls him, as though struck by a thunderbolt, from the saddle. His horse goes down. SOUND TRACK carries the sudden, triumphant yells and applause of the Saxons.

CAMERA PULLS BACK TO:

33. MED. SHOT THE SCENE
as Robin jumps from his saddle and pulls Sir Guy away

Appendix

from his horse's flailing hoofs. He then draws his sword
and waits, but Sir Guy, stunned still, is unable to arise,
though he tries. Squires, attendants, and herald gallop
out to the fallen knight. The herald looks at Sir Guy and
enters a score 'on his sheet, then he raises his trumpet
and blows. Robin, leading his horse, walks toward the
royal box.

34.   MED. SHOT   THE ROYAL BOX
The occupants are silent and chagrined.

HERALD'S VOICE:
Sir Guy of Gisbourne is unable to continue. The victor is Sir Robin of Locksley!

35.   MED. SHOT   END OF ROYAL PAVILION
Again Saxon cheers thunder out. The courier on his
bell-hung horse gallops up, pulls his horse back on its
haunches, and leaps off. He shoulders his way urgently
through the crowd, toward Prince John.

36.   MED. SHOT   ROBIN
as he walks at the head of his horse, toward the royal
box. Will of Gamwell, riding out from the side, follows
him.

37.   MED. SHOT   THE ROYAL BOX
Prince John, seated, is waiting for Robin, his face dark
with anger. Marian sits, motionless, her face set in cold
beauty. Robin walks up and halts. Salutes Prince John.

PRINCE JOHN:
Congratulations on a lucky stroke, Sir Knight!

ROBIN (cheerfully):
Lucky for Sir Guy my lance was tipped with a coro-
nel, sire, else Nottingham would need a new lord
. . . (bows to Marian) and my lady a new master!

MARIAN (flares at him):
> If that's some of your Saxon wit—

ROBIN (grins):
> You don't like it?

MARIAN (snaps):
> No more than I like Saxons!

ROBIN (shrugs, smiling):
> That's because you don't know us. We've some re-
> markable qualities . . . for instance, the art of ser-
> vility, which we've been forced to learn—(bows to
> Prince John) in good King Richard's absence.

38.   MED. CLOSE SHOT   THE GROUP
listening aghast.

ROBIN (continues cheerfully):
> You really should study us, my lady. We're easy to
> find. Just look under the heel of any Norman boot!

MARIAN (gasps):
> Why—you speak treason!

ROBIN (bows):
> Fluently!

PRINCE JOHN (thunders):
> You're overbold, Sir Robin! I'd advise you to curb
> that wagging tongue!

ROBIN (regretfully shakes his head):
> A habit I've never formed, sire!

Before Prince John can answer there is a commotion in
the box behind.

39.   MED. PAN SHOT   ROYAL BOX
as the courier thrusts forward, through the crowd toward Prince John. Prince John turns, annoyed.

PRINCE JOHN (testily):
What is it? What's the matter?

The messenger reaches him, uncovers, and drops on one knee.

CAMERA MOVES UP TO:

40. MED. CLOSE SHOT PRINCE JOHN AND MESSENGER

MESSENGER:
A message from France, Your Highness!

There is instant, tense silence. The messenger rises.

PRINCE JOHN:
From France? (Quickly.) What is it?

COURIER:
Your brother, King Richard, sire . . .

PRINCE JOHN (tense):
Go on . . . !

COURIER:
. . . on his way back to England . . . was captured in Vienna by Leopold of Austria . . . and is held prisoner in the castle of Dürenstein!

41. TWO SHOT ROBIN AND WILL OF GAMWELL
Will rides abreast of Robin, who looks up. They stare at each other in consternation.

WILL:
Robin . . . you know what that means?

ROBIN (tight-lipped):
If I didn't, *that* would soon tell me!

He jerks his head toward Prince John and group.

42. MED. CLOSE SHOT PRINCE JOHN AND GROUP
Prince John is staring at the messenger.

PRINCE JOHN (repeats as though unable to believe it):
Richard . . . a *prisoner*?

COURIER:
Yes, sire. And held in ransom of 150,000 golden
marks!

Prince John stares at him, then his crafty face breaks
into a smile. He looks around at his knights, who uncer-
tainly smile with him; then, throwing back his head,
Prince John bursts into peal after peal of loud, triumphant laughter, pauses to wipe his eyes, then roars again.
As the Normans dutifully echo him, CAMERA PULLS BACK
to show Robin and Will, their faces tense, then PANS to
a group of Saxons, as they stare at each other, murmur-
ing in terror and despair.

DISSOLVE TO:

43.   MED. SHOT   BODY SWINGING FROM GIBBET   SUNSET
The gibbet is on a hilltop. At the foot are a number of
Norman men-at-arms and a knight in full armor,
mounted, with his squire nearby. All form a grim, black
silhouette against a blood-red sky. SUPERIMPOSED is the
following title:

With King Richard a prisoner Prince John instantly
ousted the regency and, with his Norman barons,
imposed upon the helpless Saxons the most brutal,
bloody, and rapacious regime in English history.

Inventory

The following materials from the Warner library of the Wisconsin Center for Film and Theater Research were used by Behlmer in preparing *The Adventures of Robin Hood* for the Wisconsin/Warner Bros. Screenplay Series:

Temporary, by Rowland Leigh, November 23, 1936, 164 pages.
Revised Temporary, by Norman Reilly Raine, July 7, 1937, 165 pages.
Second Revised Temporary, by Raine, August 6, 1937, with changed pages to August 20, 1937, unfinished, 100 pages.
Final, by Raine and Seton I. Miller, September 4, 1937, to September 11, 1937, unfinished, 168 pages.
Revised Final, by Raine and Miller, September 14, 1937, with changed pages to September 17, 1937, 190 pages.
Second Revised Final, by Raine and Miller, September 21, 1937, 166 pages.
Third Revised Final, by Raine and Miller, no date, with changed pages to January 5, 1938, 183 pages.
Fourth Revised Final, by Raine and Miller, September 25, 1937, with changed pages (no date), 162 pages.

DESIGNED BY GARY GORE
COMPOSED BY GRAPHIC COMPOSITION, INC.
ATHENS, GEORGIA
MANUFACTURED BY INTER-COLLEGIATE PRESS, INC.
SHAWNEE MISSION, KANSAS
TEXT AND DISPLAY LINES ARE SET IN PALATINO

Library of Congress Cataloging in Publication Data
Raine, Norman Reilly, 1895–1971
The adventures of Robin Hood.
(Wisconsin/Warner Bros. screenplay series)
Screenplay by N. R. Raine and S. I. Miller.
Includes bibliographical references.
1. The adventures of Robin Hood. [Motion picture]
I. Miller, Seton I., joint author. II. Behlmer, Rudy.
III. Wisconsin Center for Film and Theater Research.
IV. Series.
PN1997.A3115R3   791.43'7   79–3971
ISBN 0–299–07940–6
ISBN 0–299–07944–9 pbk.

The Wisconsin / Warner Bros. Screenplay Series, a product of the Warner Brothers Film Library, will enable film scholars, students, researchers, and aficionados to gain insights into individual American films in ways never before possible.

The Warner library was acquired in 1957 by the United Artists Corporation, which in turn donated it to the Wisconsin Center for Film and Theater Research in 1969. The massive library, housed in the State Historical Society of Wisconsin, contains eight hundred sound feature films, fifteen hundred short subjects, and nineteen thousand still negatives, as well as the legal files, press books, and screenplays of virtually every Warner film produced from 1930 until 1950. This rich treasure trove has made the University of Wisconsin one of the major centers for film research, attracting scholars from around the world. This series of published screenplays represents a creative use of the Warner library, both a boon to scholars and a tribute to United Artists.

Most published film scripts are literal transcriptions of finished films. The Wisconsin / Warner screenplays are primary source documents—the final shooting versions including revisions made during production. As such, they will explicate the art of screenwriting as film transcriptions cannot. They will help the user to understand the arts of directing and acting, as well as the other arts involved in the film-making process, in comparing these screenplays with the final films. (Films of the Warner library are available at modest rates from the United Artists nontheatrical rental library, United Artists/16 mm.)

From the eight hundred feature films in the library, the general editor and the editorial committee of the series have chosen those that have received critical recognition for their excellence of directing, screenwriting, and acting, films that are distinctive examples of their genre, those that have particular historical relevance, and some that are adaptations of well-known novels and plays. The researcher, instructor, or student can, in the judicious selection of individual volumes for close examination, gain a heightened appreciation and broad understanding of the American film and its historical role during this critical period.